PWICH

Please return / renew by date shown.
You can renew it at:
norlink.norfolk.gov.uk
or by telephone: 0344 800 8006
Please have your library card & PIN ready

THE MYTHICAL 9th DIVISION

THE ALIEN MOON

ALEX MILWAY

WALKER
BOOKS

For William

FIRST PUBLISHED 2012 BY WALKER BOOKS LTD, 87 VAUXHALL WALK, LONDON SE11 5HJ

2 4 6 8 10 9 7 5 3 1

© 2012 ALEX MILWAY

THE RIGHT OF ALEX MILWAY TO BE IDENTIFIED AS THE AUTHOR/ILLUSTRATOR OF THIS WORK HAS BEEN ASSERTED BY HIM IN ACCORDANCE WITH THE COPYRIGHT, DESIGNS AND PATENTS ACT 1988

THIS BOOK HAS BEEN TYPESET IN ADOBE CASLON PRO AND CC DAVE GIBBONS

IMAGES OF EARTH (PAGES 130 AND 131) COURTESY OF NASA

PRINTED AND BOUND IN GREAT BRITAIN BY CLAYS LTD, ST IVES PLC

BRITISH LIBRARY CATALOGUING IN PUBLICATION DATA:
A CATALOGUE RECORD FOR THIS BOOK IS AVAILABLE FROM THE BRITISH LIBRARY

ISBN 978-1-4063-2658-1

WWW.WALKER.CO.UK
WWW.MYTHICAL9TH.COM

FOR 150 YEARS A MYSTERIOUS TRIO OF HEROIC AND RESOURCEFUL YETIS HAS EXISTED AS A *TOP SECRET* BRANCH OF THE BRITISH ARMED FORCES. OVER THE YEARS, SUCCESSIVE GENERATIONS OF YETIS HAVE WORKED FEARLESSLY TO DEFEND THE WORLD AGAINST *THE FORCES OF EVIL.* AS THESE POWERS GROW EVER DEADLIER, THE YETIS FIGHT ON, PITTING BOTH *STRENGTH* AND *WITS* AGAINST THE MIGHT OF THEIR ENEMIES.

THEY ARE THE MYTHICAL 9TH DIVISION.

ALBRECHT

AS THE LEADER OF THE MYTHICAL 9TH DIVISION, ALBRECHT IS INTELLIGENT, QUICK-WITTED AND DEDICATED TO THE CAUSE. UNLIKE MOST YETIS, ALBRECHT MAINTAINS A GREAT INTEREST IN TECHNOLOGY, AND KEEPS UP TO DATE WITH THE LATEST GADGETS.

TIMONEN

THE LARGEST YETI EVER TO HAVE GRACED THE EARTH, TIMONEN IS A GIANT AMONG GIANTS. HIS HEARTFELT LOVE OF YAKS FREQUENTLY LANDS HIM IN TROUBLE, BUT WHAT HE LACKS IN TACT AND INTELLIGENCE, HE MAKES UP FOR IN SHEER STRENGTH.

SAAR

THE MOST EXPERIENCED OF THE MYTHICAL 9TH DIVISION, SAAR CAN ALWAYS BE IDENTIFIED IN A LINE-UP BY HIS LONG STRIPY SCARF. HE'S CLEVER, THOUGHTFUL AND ONE OF THE LAST YETIS IN THE WORLD TO FOLLOW THE MYSTICAL WAY OF THE YETI.

Prologue

THE SURFACE OF THE MOON:
238,957 MILES FROM EARTH

MEANWHILE ON CAPTAIN PONKERTON'S DESK

For their achievements in the field, the yetis are to be honoured with the Congressional Gold Medal. Albrecht, Timonen and Saar of the Mythical 9th Division are cordially invited to attend a secret ceremony at Camp David, where President Abak Orama will present them with the highest accolade afforded to yetis by the United States of America.

THE MYTHICAL 9th DIVISION

Chapter 1: The "More Secret than Top Secret" Mission

15

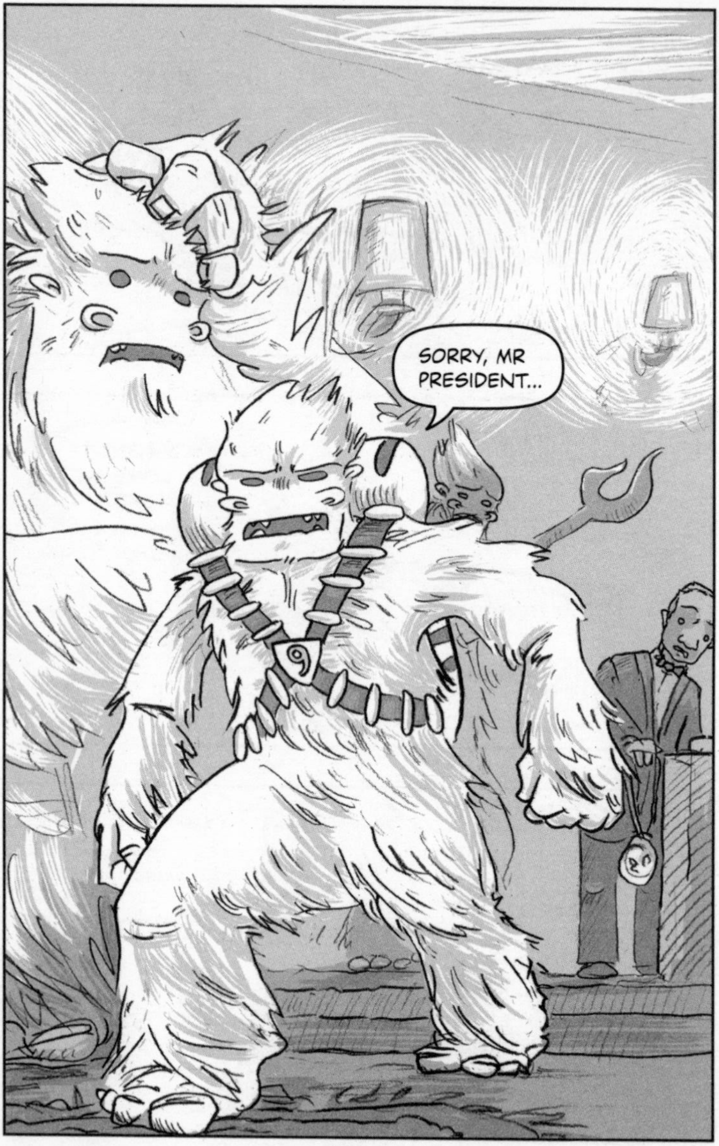
SORRY, MR PRESIDENT...

"What now?" said Albrecht to Captain Ponkerton.

"It's an emergency so top secret not even I know about it," said Ponkerton. "Sherpa I's ready for you."

Albrecht looked at the president and muttered, "Sorry," again in a very apologetic voice. "This

IT'S AN EMERGENCY.

doesn't normally happen," he added.

Timonen snatched his medal from the bewildered President. He looped its ribbon over his massive head but it wouldn't slide past his eyebrows.

"Stupid thing," said the giant yeti. He threw it to the ground and marched off through the room.

"Sorry about him," said Saar, tightening his scarf. "He gets angry when he's hungry."

"Don't let me get in your way," said the President, looking a little baffled.

"We won't," said Timonen.

The three yetis left the room and were escorted out of the building by military guards. Sherpa I was waiting on the neatly trimmed lawn of Camp David, its engines chugging over.

"So where are we going?" said Timonen, clambering inside the aeroplane.

"Your guess is as good as mine," said Albrecht.

He waited for Saar to climb in, then waved at the President and sealed the door.

"Please take your seats," requested ROLF, the onboard computer.

The yetis buckled their safety belts and Sherpa I roared into the sky, tearing deep ruts in the grass.

"ROLF," said Albrecht, "what's our destination?"

The onboard computer beeped.

"The destination is not in my databank," said ROLF. "I am being piloted remotely."

"If you're not busy, then," said Timonen, "you can cook me some lunch."

"There are pizzas in the microwave below your seat," said ROLF.

"It was anticipated that you would be suffering from hunger."

Timonen's stomach made happy noises.

"So if *you* don't know where we're headed," said Saar, "then who does?"

"That information is not available to me," said ROLF.

"Any indication of arrival time?" asked Albrecht.

"I have roughly four hours and twenty six minutes of fuel," said ROLF.

"That's not enough to leave the United States," said Saar.

Timonen was totally disinterested in their conversation. Two slices of pizza were halfway into his mouth, and melted cheese was dripping onto the floor.

"Just tell me when we get there," he said, slouching back and closing his eyes.

Deep underground, in a bunker far below the Nevada desert, Solomon Grundy was poring over a video transmission from outer space.

"This is looking more suitable by the minute," he said. "It is exactly as I'd hoped."

He lifted his eye patch to reveal a hidden robotic eye with super zoom functionality. Its dials and lenses flicked and whirred as Grundy focused on the images.

"In the right hands, it could be the most sinister weapon of all time," he said. He smiled to himself. "And would you believe it? My hands *are* the right hands."

Grundy heard footsteps approaching his office. He slid the eye patch back over his robotic eye.

"Captain Grundy, sir!" said a masked soldier.

The soldiers of Compound W had been built specifically for their jobs by the scientists at the base. They were cyborgs, half-human half-robot, and contained cloned elements of Solomon Grundy within their DNA. They were perfect for top secret jobs as they posed no security threat and answered to Grundy alone.

"Yes?" said Grundy.

"The last of the Divisions is about to land," said the soldier. "We're nearly ready for you."

"Thank you," said Grundy. He stood up and realigned his black suit and tie. "Let's get this show on the road."

* * *
*

Four hours and five minutes later, Sherpa I began its descent.

Through the tiny window, Albrecht saw a dusty, mountainous landscape.

"Looks inviting," he said, sarcastically. "ROLF, state our location."

"Nevada," said the computer, "thirty kilometres east of Death Valley."

"I can see why they kept that one from us," said Saar.

"Preparing to land," said the computer. Sherpa I's airbrakes fired into action and with three controlled bumps the craft landed on a runway in an ancient dried-up lake.

"Right," said Albrecht, leaving his seat, "Let's see what's out there."

He tried to push the door open, but it wouldn't budge.

"I apologize," said ROLF, "but the doors are locked and can only be opened externally."

"By whom?" said Saar.

"I do not have that information," said ROLF.

"Get me Ponkerton!" said Albrecht. "This is ridiculous."

"I cannot," said ROLF. "My communication systems are blocked."

"Who has the power to do this?" said Saar.

"Vehicle approaching," said ROLF.

"This sounds too weird to me," said Albrecht.

He stretched up into a cabinet and found a rectangular box labelled, IN CASE OF EMERGENCY LANDING AT SEA. Inside were three stubby cylindrical syringes. He passed one to each of his friends, then held his own against his leg.

"Do it," said Albrecht.

All three yetis yelped as they clicked the top of the syringe and a small pinprick broke their skin.

"Just in case anything happens," said Albrecht. "Ponkerton can find our positions with these homing chips."

"I've just injected myself with chips?" said Timonen angrily.

"I could have eaten them!"

"Don't be ridiculous," said Albrecht. "They're tiny digital homing beacons."

"How depressing," said Saar. "I can never get lost again."

"It's just a precaution," said Albrecht, seriously.

"Ooh, look," said Timonen, pointing out of the window.

"We've got company."

A black-windowed bus pulled up outside. Six soldiers dressed all in black, their faces shielded by darkened visors, leaped to the ground and ran to Sherpa I. With a hiss of escaping air, the door opened.

"Just what is this?" said Albrecht angrily, staring into the soldiers' faceless masks.

"We don't answer questions," came the reply from the soldier closest to him. "Follow us to the compound."

"Compound?" said Albrecht. He looked about him and could see only mountains and desert.

"Your questions will be answered there," said the guard.

Timonen pushed Albrecht out of Sherpa I and stepped down to the ground. He towered over the soldiers, but as far as he could tell they were unmoved by his terrifying size.

"Want me to sort them out?" he said.

Saar slipped down and found that the air was hot and dry.

"If we don't go with them," he said, wisely, "in this heat, we'll shrivel up like raisins."

A soldier moved them along.

"Please step into the vehicle and remove any items you're

wearing," he said.

"I'm not giving you my backpack," said Albrecht.

"It's procedure," said the soldier. "To enter the compound everything must be processed and decontaminated."

"Decontaminated?" said Albrecht.

"You heard me," said the soldier.

"Can you decontaminate Timonen while you're at it?" said Saar.

"Can you shut up?" said Timonen.

"You will all undergo rigorous cleansing treatments," said the soldier. "No foreign matter can be allowed to enter the compound."

"Cleansing treatments?" said Timonen. "If any nit-nurse touches me, I'll bite their hands off."

"Please," said the soldier, hurrying things along. "We are running out of time."

Albrecht sighed, and the yetis reluctantly removed their kit and boarded the bus.

The windows were blacked out and, when the doors shut, the outside world was completely cut off.

"Everyone take a seat," said the driver as the bus jerked forwards. "Arrival time at Compound W is 300 seconds."

Five minutes later, the bus dropped sharply downwards and there was a sound of metal doors clanging shut. The bus had reached its destination.

"Decontamination awaits," said a soldier bluntly, opening the door.

The yetis walked out into a huge aircraft hangar, filled with military weapons and combat vehicles of every kind, from massive bomber planes to armoured jeeps.

"Wow!" said Albrecht. "Good job you lot are on our side."

"This isn't a sightseeing trip," said the soldier. "Follow me to your place of decontamination."

The soldier marched off along a painted yellow walkway, and the yetis kept close. The remaining soldiers filed out of the bus carrying the yetis' gear and disappeared into a far-off doorway.

"Do not deviate from the path," said the lead soldier.

"Or what?" said Timonen. He dangled his toe over the walkway and a deafening siren squealed overhead. As soon as he stepped back the noise stopped.

"Or we'll all go deaf," said Saar.

Albrecht nudged Timonen.

"Don't be childish," he said.

"URGH!" said Timonen. He pushed his toe over the walkway's edge and the alarms sang again.

The lead soldier stopped and turned around with his gun at the ready.

"Do that again and I'll neutralize you," he said. "I don't care what or who you are, but when you're in Compound W you're under my command."

Albrecht pointed a stern finger at Timonen, who pushed it away and continued walking.

"You need to work on your angry finger," said Saar, laughing.

"It's no fun being the division leader when your team spend all their time laughing at you," Albrecht grumbled.

Eventually they reached a round metal door, which opened silently and of its own accord.

"Decontamination Room 3," said the soldier. "Here's where I leave you."

The cold, steel room was empty but for three tall stools.

"Take a seat," said a voice, booming out from a tannoy, "and the decon process will start."

Timonen looked puzzled.

"They're having a laugh if they expect me to wash myself," he said.

"With what?" said Saar. "I don't see any water."

Albrecht looked around the empty room but found nothing.

"Weird," he said.

With a *fizz* and a *shush*, blue gas started seeping from the base of the stools.

"That worries me," said Saar.

"It's nothing to worry about," said a voice. "This gas is harmless to yet-is. It will eradicate any spores, mites or other bugs that you might be harbouring."

"I beg your pardon?" said Albrecht with indignation. He peered at his feet as the blue gas swirled around his body. Tiny black spots of what looked like dust were falling from his fur to the floor.

"Fleas of a yak!" he said.

"Actually, it's a mixture of fleas, ticks and lice," said the voice.

Albrecht was highly embarrassed. But he felt significantly better when he saw the mound of dead creatures about Timonen's knees. Saar had just three small specks of black below his stool.

"At least one of us understands the importance of grooming," said Saar.

"Yes, Mum," said Timonen. He kicked through his pile of bugs as if they were fallen leaves, scattering them everywhere. He kicked through his pile of bugs as if they were fallen leaves, scattering them everywhere. The grate in the floor opened. The yetis felt the pull of a giant vacuum cleaner against their fur, and the dead bugs whizzed off into the hole.

Once the gas dissipated, a grate in the floor opened. The yetis felt the pull of a giant vacuum cleaner against their fur, and the dead bugs whizzed off into the hole.

"Yetis, you are now clean and ready to enter the base," said the tannoy voice.

A door opened in the wall and a tall man dressed from head to toe in black walked inside. He had an eye patch covering

his right eye, and his jet black hair was smeared down across his fringe with grease.

"Good afternoon, yetis," he said with a slight sneer. It was his voice the yetis had heard within the room. "My name is Solomon Grundy, head of the Mythical 7th Division."

"Aha!" said Albrecht. "Now it all makes sense."

"Very little in this world makes sense," said Grundy imperiously. "And what you are about to see and experience in Compound W is highly classified. Do not speak a word of it or we shall be forced to wipe your memories."

"Compound W is a bag of nonsense," replied Timonen. Grundy slid creepily towards Timonen and pointed at his nose.

"Believe me," said Grundy, "the building you're standing in does not exist. I do not exist. Now, with your arrival, everyone is present and correct. Please come with me to the briefing room."

THE MYTHICAL **9th** DIVISION

Chapter 2: Testing Times

IN COMPOUND W, SOLOMON GRUNDY LEADS THE YETIS TO AN AUDITORIUM

TAKE A SEAT WITH THE OTHERS.

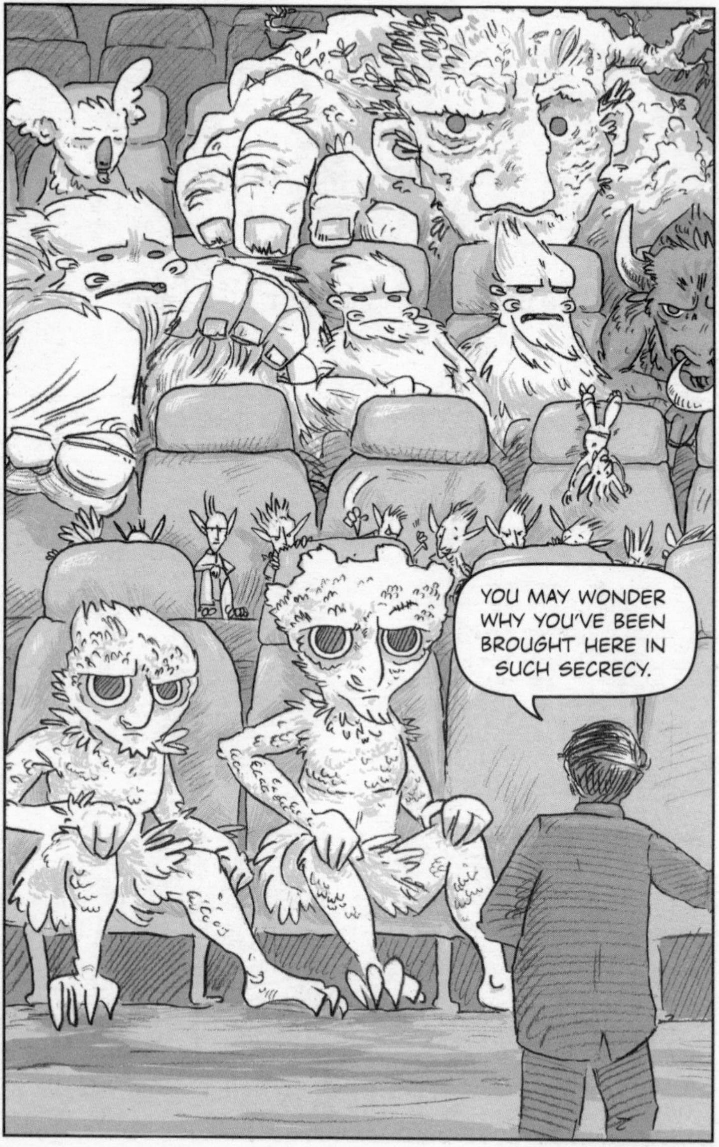
YOU MAY WONDER WHY YOU'VE BEEN BROUGHT HERE IN SUCH SECRECY.

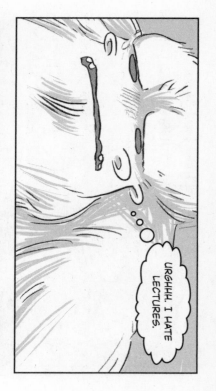

"Ohhh," said Albrecht.

"All I'll say," said Grundy, "is that the mission is to save a rare species."

A hush descended over the room. It finally sounded important.

"Okay," muttered Saar. "Now this is sounding interesting."

"You would say that," said Timonen. "We might be saving some sludge bug that lives on yak dung."

I CANNOT TELL YOU!

"I thought you liked yaks?" said Albrecht.

"Yaks and poo bugs are very different matters," said Timonen.

"To find out which, if any, of you hardened troops are built for the mission, you are all to be subject to a series of challenging secret tests," said Grundy.

There was a loud mumbling of discontent around the room.

Three minotaurs bellowed loudly.

"I'm not sitting any tests," moaned Timonen.

"And if he says 'secret' again," said Saar, "I'm walking out."

"You all," said Grundy, "will be pushed to your limits. You may faint, vomit, and even mess yourself…"

"A normal day for Timonen, then," said Saar.

Timonen leant over Albrecht and punched Saar on the leg.

"The first test will begin in twenty minutes," said Grundy. "Please make your way to the front of the auditorium and we'll go from there."

"If any of these tests involve maths," said Timonen, "I'm going home."

"I can't imagine we're here for a maths test," said Saar.

"Come on," said Albrecht, enjoying the challenge, "it'll be like being back at training camp."

"And that was rubbish," said Timonen, moaning.

The yetis waited for their first task to be assigned. They were queuing behind four minotaurs who, as Timonen found out, emitted a strong whiff of manure wherever they went.

"You're allowed to wash," said Timonen, holding his nose. The minotaurs swivelled on their hooves. Their muscle-bound torsos bulged like overblown balloons. The heavy metal hoops hanging through their noses rattled on Timonen's chest and spit splattered his fur as they snorted into his face.

"POOOOO!" he yelled. "And your breath reeks!"

"Well I never," said Saar. "Timonen has an opinion on personal hygiene."

"I must apologize for my friend," said Albrecht, greeting the minotaurs with a handshake. The minotaurs were positively rippling with muscles, and their grip was the sort that could tear your arm from its socket.

"My name is Magnus," said one of the minotaurs, in a gruff voice. "Your friend has insulted our honour."

"He does that," said Albrecht. "I'm really sorry."

"We minotaurs do not forgive slights to our honour," said Magnus.

"Just this once?" asked Albrecht, pleading.

"No," said Magnus.

He turned away and a huge troll walked in between them. Albrecht was faced with its bark-covered shoulder.

"Well done, Timonen," said Albrecht. "How many more enemies are you planning on making today?"

"Those pumped up cows are all show," said Timonen. "They should be mooing in a field, leave saving the world to the big guys."

A man in a black lab coat counted the creatures and split them into groups. The three yetis, along with a lumbering troll and six green-skinned goblins were then taken down a corridor

and led into a vast circular hall. They were asked to step in-side a tear-shaped vehicle, which was attached to a machine in the centre of the hall by a long arm. No bigger than a minibus, there were two rows of seats squeezed inside.

"Move in and sit down," said the man. "Once you're settled, strap yourself in."

Albrecht led the way and took the first seat.

"It's like going to the cinema," he said, sliding down between the cushioned arms.

The seat had a large headrest, and the guard set its height before attaching a circular probe to Albrecht's chest. Once eve-ryone was locked in place, the guard flicked a switch to turn on the onboard monitors.

"Test one, underway," said the man, stepping from the vehicle. He slammed shut the door, cranked a wheel to lock it and walked off to a viewing room within the walls of the hall. The passengers sat silently, staring through a window at the front of the vehicle.

"What's this all about, then?" said Timonen.

"I've got no idea," said Albrecht.

THE MYTHICAL 9TH DIVISION 41 The Alien Moon

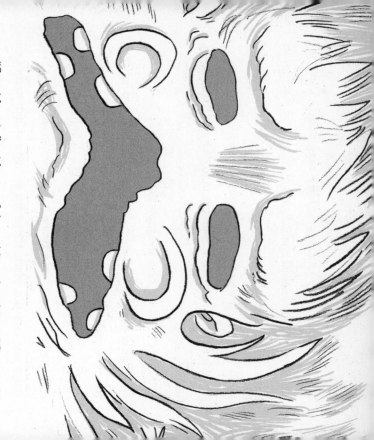

"Stupid yetis," said one of the goblins, laughing. "Get ready for g-force!"

"What's g-force?" said Timonen.

"Oh dear," said Albrecht. "Hold tight…"

The vehicle shuddered, then slowly circled the huge hall in majestic sweeps. The yetis felt their heads pull back onto the headrests as the vehicle sped up.

"Trolls don't like this sort of thing," said the troll, shakily.

"I'm ... not ... sure ... yetis ... do ... either," said Albrecht, feeling his face spread out across the headrest like ice cream melting into a bowl.

"Breathe ... deeply," said Saar, reassuring himself. He closed his eyes.

Timonen's mouth was now pulled wider than his face, his lips flapping back over his eyes.

"AHhh BleH JAAA!" he said.

The goblins burst into laughter. They were loving it. The troll felt its face seize up, its eyeballs squeezed to near bursting point, and it passed out.

"One down!" squealed the goblins, laughing harder and harder. "FASTER! FASTER!"

Timonen's massive bulk wobbled like a plate of jelly against his chair. Each circuit of the hall revealed more of the insides of his mouth.

"Tchump!" muttered Timonen, before he too passed out.

"Two down!" squealed the goblins.

"Calm..." said Saar.

"Can't do it..." said Albrecht. His breathing sped up, his eyesight failed and he also passed out.

"Threeeeeeee!" cried the goblins, but it was too much even for them. They slumped back into their chairs, out cold.

Saar breathed deeply, meditating as peacefully as he could manage under the circumstances. His head felt as though it was floating high above his shoulders, his hands miles away in a distant country and his feet far below the sea.

As he was imagining blue skies and little fluffy clouds, the vehicle stopped accelerating and began its long journey back to a standstill.

Saar opened his eyes. Things were all a bit blurry and too tinged with purple for his liking, but he was fine. He sniffed and rubbed his nose.

"Oh!" he said, looking around. "What's happened to everyone?"

The next test took place in a long, cylindrical chamber, coloured in black and white stripes. A scientist opened a door in the glass and walked through.

"I want you all to enter and find a good footing on one of these stripes," he said. "One person per stripe."

"What's going to happen?" asked Saar, frowning as he looked around the chamber.

"We must maintain an element of surprise," said the scientist over his shoulder, retreating to the viewing room. He closed the door on them and the troll looked set to burst into tears.

"Are you all comfortable?" asked the guard over a tannoy.

The goblins looked at each other and giggled uncontrollably.

The scientists switched on the machine that was hidden

inside the chamber. The ground beneath Albrecht's feet moved backwards, sliding along like a travelator at an airport.

"Keep walking to maintain your balance!" said a scientist.

"This is a test of your stamina."

The travelator sped up gradually until everyone was running frantically on the spot. The yetis found this incredibly easy because their legs were long enough to cope with the speed with little hassle. The goblins, however, kept falling over their feet. They happily kept getting back up and carrying on. It was all too much effort for the troll, who had taken to weeping like a willow.

"Okay!" said a scientist. "Keep focused. We're increasing the speed."

The travelator was now zipping along at an incredible rate. The troll missed its footing and was sent rocketing into the far wall. The goblins soon followed. All the while, the scientists made notes of everyone's progress.

The floor slowed to a stop and a strange hum filled the room. All five sides of the chamber glowed bright blue as the troll and goblins struggled back to the front of the room.

"And finally," said a scientist, "if you'd all head back to your starting positions."

"This might shock you initially," said a scientist. "Just try to stay calm and maintain your positions."

Albrecht looked at Saar, who was sweating profusely.

"What next?" said Albrecht.

Even as he said the words, he felt his feet lift off the floor and he realized he was floating in midair.

"They've turned off the gravity!" said Saar.

Albrecht's stomach turned over as his legs rose up above his head. He held his arms out to find a balance, eventually clasping hold of Saar to steady himself. Saar was the epitome of calm and his body stayed in one spot at all times.

"If you need to be sick," said the scientist. "Please try to hold it in."

"WOOOOAH!" said Timonen.

The heaviest, and last to be affected by the anti-gravity machine, Timonen drifted off and squashed three goblins against a wall. The goblins couldn't have been happier and continued to giggle.

"Please, stop…" whimpered the troll. He was upside down on the ceiling, his wizened fingers gripping the metal ceiling panels.

"Anti-gravity?" said Saar quietly. "This can only mean one thing."

"I'm thinking the same," said Albrecht.

"Space..." they said in unison.

A scientist nodded to his colleague in the control room.

"Good!" he said. "Prepare for landing."

The blue lights in the walls dimmed and everyone sank softly to the floor.

A scientist opened the door and invited the test subjects to leave.

"You'll be pleased to know that this is last of the physical tests," he said.

The troll burst into tears again. The goblins looked annoyed.

"The next test will be mental," said a scientist.

"They've all been mental," said Timonen.

"I think he means they're going to test our brains," said Saar.

"A waste of time where you're concerned."

"Yes," said the scientist, "the next test will work your mental agility to its limit. Please follow me."

"How are the recruits faring?" asked Grundy.

He was standing in a high security munitions dump, surrounded

by hundreds of waist-high missiles. A scientist flicked through his notes, revealing the welfare of the test subjects.

"We have barely any that are suitable for space flight," said the scientist.

"Don't weigh too heavily on that priority," said Grundy. "This mission is more about dedication and commitment. We need at least one of them to return with the goods."

"Then there are definitely three or four who might have what it takes," said the scientist.

"Good," said Grundy.

He unlocked the tip of one of the rockets and unscrewed it from its base. It was empty and ready for its payload.

"What are these made of?" he asked.

"Carbon fibres," said the scientist.

"And the distance they can travel?" asked Grundy.

"Up to a thousand miles, depending on conditions."

"They sound perfect," said Grundy. "Have them moved to the cargo bay. We should be as ready as we can."

"I'll make it so," said the scientist.

"Once the mission is underway," said Grundy, "raise our defence

status to Red Alert and put Compound W on lockdown."

"Yes, sir," said the scientist.

"And block external transmissions," said Grundy. "No word is to get in or out of this base once the wheels are in motion."

"Of course, sir," said the scientist.

Grundy was clearly starting to get excited.

"Get the tests finished," he said. "The sooner we know what's out there, the sooner we can take over the world."

"I told you, I'm not doing any maths test," said Timonen, as he sat down beside Albrecht for their final test. The room was bright and paper and pens were laid out on every desk.

"I doubt you'll get lunch without it," said Albrecht cunningly.

Timonen rethought his approach.

"As long as I don't have to get anything right, then," he said.

"Oh, Timonen," said Saar patronizingly. "I can't imagine anyone really expects you to."

"Shush," said the scientist, walking up and down the rows. "I request silence throughout. The test lasts thirty minutes, and I expect all of you to do your best."

A scrumpled piece of paper hit the troll on the head. He turned slowly in his chair and caught sight of the goblins readying a second missile. He began to cry again.

The goblins sniggered and picked up their pens.

The scientist put a question sheet on each desk and then started a stopwatch.

"The test starts now," he said.

Timonen had bitten the end off his pen and ink was flowing down his beard.

"Can I have a new one?" he asked, holding the shattered pen aloft.

The scientist had the unnerving feeling of being a schoolteacher in front of an unruly class.

"I'll get you one now," he sighed.

Albrecht, like the good student he was, had made a start. The first question, however, had him stumped.

It was going to be a long half-hour.

Saar focused on the task at hand and read through the questions. The clock ticked away.

After ten minutes, the goblins had started eating their

desks, pulling away metallic parts and throwing them at the troll. Fifteen minutes in, the troll stood up and left the room in tears. By twenty minutes, Timonen was fast asleep and Albrecht and Saar were the only two labouring away. By the end of the half-hour, it was only Saar who thought that he might have got one answer right.

"STOP!" cried the scientist.

Timonen sat bolt upright in his chair and the goblins sat bolt upright on the floor as they'd eaten their chairs. The scientist collected the two answer papers from Albrecht and Saar.

"Thank you for your patience," he said. "You may return to the auditorium and get yourselves some lunch."

"At last," said Timonen. "Has anyone else ever noticed that eating pens just makes you feel hungrier?"

The auditorium was heaving with mythical creatures when Solomon Grundy returned with the test results.

A silence fell over the mythical beasts. Grundy looked along the rows of seats and began to speak.

"You have all displayed the attributes that make you key players in the constant global struggle against evil", he said.

"Unfortunately, only one of you has displayed the abilities necessary to undergo this most secret of missions."

There was a clear lack of enthusiasm in the room. Most of the creatures looked pale and exhausted.

"So please," said Solomon Grundy, "could Saar, of the Mythical 9th Division step forward. The rest of you will be returned to your homelands."

"Huh?" croaked Timonen. "Him?!"

Saar flicked a stare at Albrecht.

"I'm not going anywhere without you two," he said, standing up. "One for all and all for one, eh?" He walked down to see Grundy and Albrecht and Timonen followed.

"You are a unique soldier," said Grundy, eyeing Saar and ignoring the other two. "In fact I'd go so far as saying you're

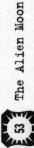

the most impressive specimen I've ever conducted tests on."

"Specimen?" said Saar.

"Creature, I mean," added Grundy. "Your results were quite unexpected for a yeti."

"Let's be clear," said Saar firmly. "I don't know what's going on here, but I'm not undertaking any mission without my team."

Grundy itched the eyebrow above his eye patch.

"I presume you mean these two?" he said.

"I do," replied Saar.

Grundy paused for a few seconds, eyeing up Timonen. His size could be problematic to the mission. He weighed up the options. If the mission was to be successful, he had to have Saar.

"So be it," said Grundy. "You'll get your wish and your team."

"Good," said Saar. "Now you're going to have to tell me what this ridiculous mission is all about."

"Prepare to be amazed," said Grundy. "Your world will never be the same again."

THE MYTHICAL 9th DIVISION

Chapter 3: The Narg

THE YETIS ARE SHOWN TO A SECRET HANGAR DOOR

OPERATIVE 612, YOU CAN COME IN NOW!

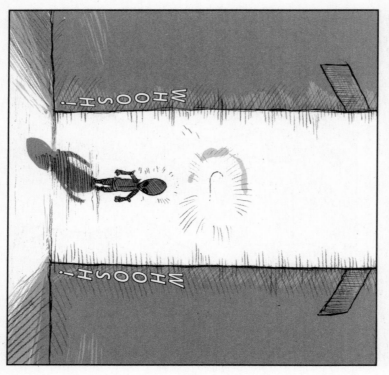

56

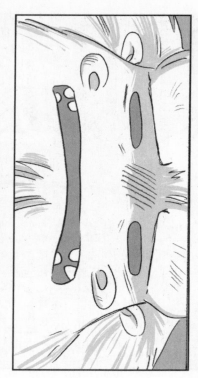

Grundy held his hand high in greeting then turned back to the yetis.

"What you have just witnessed will change the way you see the world forever," he said.

"Now you understand the reason for my secrecy. We couldn't let just anyone know about this mission."

"But this means ..." said Saar, the momentous occasion getting the

IT'S AN **ALIEN!**

better of him, "the universe has life elsewhere..."

Oola held up a three-fingered hand in greeting, then spoke.

"⠇⠽⠵⠪⠗⠈⠺⠙ ⠙⠙⠽⠽⠪ ⠙⠽⠪⠕⠙⠽⠙⠪⠙

"⠇⠁⠁ ⠙⠪⠽⠈⠙⠙⠡"

"He's talking nonsense!" said Timonen.

"He's a she," said Grundy.

"Owww!" shouted Timonen, twisting his fingers into his temples. "What's happening to me?"

Timonen's head felt hot, as though it was burning up on the inside.

"Wait," said Grundy, smiling.

Timonen's eyes rolled around in their sockets. His thoughts of steak and fries vanished from his brain and a stream of brightly coloured imagery and words leaped into his mind.

"O great hairy one," said Oola. "The Narg are honoured to meet you."

Timonen looked at Albrecht and Saar with the expression of a stunned turnip.

"Did you hear that?" he said.

"Oola needed to connect her mind with yours," said Grundy. "Your thought patterns are now linked, so you'll understand what she says."

Oola approached Albrecht and Saar, letting her thoughts combine with theirs.

"Mountain creatures, you have come to save my race," said Oola. "The Narg thank you."

"Amazing," said Saar, hearing Oola's words for the first time.

"It was like my mind underwent a thorough spring-clean."

"And was filled with alien furniture," added Albrecht.

Grundy clapped his hands.

"Now we've got that out of the way," he said, "we must brief you on the mission. There is little time to waste."

The lights dimmed behind Oola, revealing a large spaceship. Constructed of a bulging horizontal disc with a spherical centre, the ship resembled the planet Saturn and its rings. It was raised above the floor on eight spindly metal legs and a staircase descended from its undercarriage.

"Oola is a representative of the Narg on planet Earth," said Grundy. "As members of the Mythical 7th Division, the Narg have helped us understand the cosmos."

"So where are the others?" asked Saar.

"That is the very reason we brought you here," said Grundy. "This compound is part of a facility known to the outside world as Area 51. It is the Space Research and Development arm of the Mythical 7th Division. It does not exist to you, or to anyone else, and it never will."

"What?" said Timonen.

"Just don't tell anyone about it," said Saar, bemused by all the secrecy.

"In 1947," said Grundy, "when Oola and her kind crashed near Roswell, they needed refuge. We gave them sanctuary, shielding them from the world."

"Humans showed us great kindness," said Oola.

"And to repay us, they joined the 7th Division," added Grundy.

"Human knowledge was small," said Oola. "It still is small." Saar smiled.

"I am inclined to agree with you," he said.

Grundy lifted his nose and sniffed grumpily.

"Human brains, in some areas, have improved greatly since then," he stated. "Yet this talk diverts us from our mission."

"Yeah," said Timonen. "And you're all being boring."

Grundy continued.

"Our gravity soon proved too great for the Narg," he said. "We had to find an alternative home…"

"Your Moon," announced Oola, clutching the air. "The great Ogragog!"

"They name everything after their homeland," said Grundy.

"So there are aliens on the Moon?" asked Albrecht.

"You're quick for a lesser primate," said Grundy. "The Apollo missions were instigated to transport the Narg to safety."

"But I watched those on TV!" said Saar.

"As did most of the world," said Grundy. "With a little help from Nargian knowledge, the Apollo missions successfully landed the Narg, and humans, on the Moon. They became a vital outpost to our division's work."

"Incredible," said Saar. "But how have they remained unnoticed?"

"The Narg built a low gravity base out of sight and detection of humans," said Grundy. "Which brings us to the heart of the matter. We've lost contact with the Moonbase."

Oola placed her hand on her chest.

"I have had no signal from Ogragog for three Earth days," she said.

"And you want us to go and find out why," said Albrecht.

"You'd be an expeditionary force to support Oola," said Grundy.

"The Narg are far too valuable to LEGENDS to let them die."

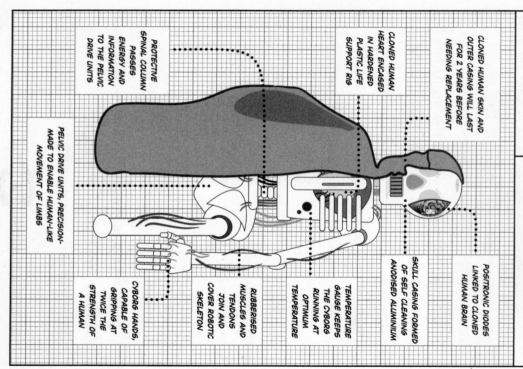

Albrecht's eyes glazed over.

"I'll be the first yeti on the Moon," he said excitedly, already thinking of important things to say as he took his first steps.

"I'm in, when do we leave?"

"What's the food like up there?" asked Timonen.

"Space food?" said Grundy. "There's nothing like it."

"Now that's what I'm talking about," said Timonen, his interest piqued.

"So what now?" said Saar.

Grundy pressed his communicator and called for his team.

"A small amount of measuring, and you'll be ready for space travel," he said.

A door opened and in marched a team of scientists carrying spacesuits. One of the suits was the size of a house and just perfect for Timonen.

"Remember," said Grundy. "We have no idea what you might encounter on the Moon. With no signal, we have no visuals. All comms are dead."

"That sounds like a normal mission for us," said Albrecht.

"We're the best team for the job."

"I can see that you are," said Grundy, patting Albrecht on the back.

He walked away, scheming to himself.

"The perfect tools for the job…" he mumbled.

"Pardon?" said Albrecht. "What did you say?"

"Oh, nothing," said Grundy. "You'll do LEGENDS proud."

After some tinkering and spot-welding of the suits, the yetis looked ready for space.

"Luke Skywalker eat your heart out," said Albrecht, stretching his arms.

The cream and red outfits were tight and Albrecht looked at his reflection in one of the brushed metal walls of the hangar. He'd never felt so dapper. Even the smooth metal backpack containing their life support was cool.

"Do my eyes deceive me?" said Saar. "Timonen looks … well … thin."

Timonen's suit flattened many of his bumps and rounded him out into a fairly flattering shape.

"If you went on a diet you'd look like that all the time," added Saar.

"I've got big bones," grumbled Timonen, but even he was impressed with his newly reduced curves.

"And here are your helmets," said Grundy.

He handed them to the yetis and demonstrated how to secure one on Albrecht.

"Click, clunk," said Grundy, sliding the bullet-shaped helmet down over Albrecht's head and twisting it into place. "Those noises mean you've created an airtight seal."

Two dull, blue lights switched on inside the visor of Albrecht's helmet to signal the connection was good.

"Oola breathes our air," said Grundy, "so you'll only need to wear the helmets when on the Moon."

"Anything else we need to know?" asked Saar.

"You have ten hours' supply of air in your backpacks," said Grundy. "Those two lights inside your helmet will turn red when you have just one hour left."

"Do we get laser guns?" asked Timonen.

"I'm afraid not," said Grundy. "Firearms are banned."

Three scientists appeared from the spaceship's staircase and signalled to Grundy that it was ready.

"The supplies are on board," said Grundy, "which means we're all set."

"What about our things?" asked Albrecht.

"Your equipment is inside waiting for you," he replied. "And you'll also need this."

He handed Albrecht his RoAR.

"My scientists have adapted it for space. The signal is boosted and you'll find it easier to contact me when on the Moon."

"Wow," said Albrecht. "A deep space communicator! I should call Captain Ponkerton and tell him what we're up to."

"That won't be necessary," said Grundy. "I'm in close contact with High Command."

"You'll let him know?" asked Albrecht.

"He already knows," said Grundy, scratching his eyebrow. "Now, if you'd like to step aboard we can prepare for launch."

"Lunch?" said Timonen, hopefully.

"Launch," said Grundy.

The yetis walked cautiously towards the spaceship and climbed

the short distance up into the craft. The lights were low, making it hard to see much of the interior, but Oola was standing at the top of the staircase.

"Make Tala your home," she said. "Love her and she will love you."

"Tala?" said Timonen.

"I think she means her ship," said Saar.

Once the yetis were inside, Oola raised a hand, communicating with the craft. With a tiny shiver, the staircase folded up and sealed the spaceship.

"How did you do that?" asked Albrecht.

"Tala listens to me," said Oola. "We have been friends for many years."

"Not even Saar can close doors with his mind!" said Albrecht.

"Is that why you aliens have such big heads?" asked Timonen.

"Our brains are three times more powerful than human brains," said Oola.

"And ten times more powerful than Timonen's," said Saar.

"But he *is* very furry," said Oola. "I am not."

"That is true," said Saar.

Oola scampered off down a long corridor. The spaceship interior was colourful, with unusual artwork covering the walls.

"Please," said Oola, turning, "speed is a necessity."

The yetis followed her onto a circular flight deck, which had a massive metal orb at its centre. It hummed with energy.

"This is the heart of my ship," said Oola, pressing her hand against the orb. "It is the power and the mind of Tala."

A screen appeared on the far wall bearing an image of the inside of the hangar.

"Breathe deeply," said Oola taking her place at the front of the deck, sitting on a tall hand-shaped chair. "Your ears may sting."

Oola tapped some controls and the hum of the orb grew louder. Blue lights glowed from the edges of the walls. The ship lurched upwards and rocked a little before settling into a calm hover.

"Open hangar," said Oola.

The ceiling of the hangar opened, revealing blue sky over Area 51.

"We are coming for you," said Oola. She looked at each yeti.

"Furry friends, space awaits us."

The orb rumbled, and in a flash of blue light, the spaceship leapt into the skies.

The headquarters of the Mythical 7th Division was the most secretive place on Earth and very few people knew what went on inside its walls. Even those who did had no idea of what Solomon Grundy was planning. His time as a loyal servant of LEGENDS was about to come to an end.

He marched back towards his office, passing through the deep space experimentation laboratory on the way. There were unusual moon rocks and meteorites, alien spores and astronaut bones housed in specimen jars and glass cabinets. All of them had been dissected and examined in minute detail. All of them had proved invaluable to Grundy's masterplan.

For many years, Grundy had been biding his time, but now the power at his fingertips was too much to ignore. The yetis were about to discover something that could make him the most powerful man on Earth.

"Now to sit back and watch," he said.

He entered his office and cast his eyes over a large multi-screen display. It pulled in feeds from the numerous satellites focused solely on the Moon's surface. He'd lied when he said there was no signal.

"Come on yetis," he said. "Make me happy."

THE MYTHICAL **9**th DIVISION

Chapter 4: Transcending
to Outer Space

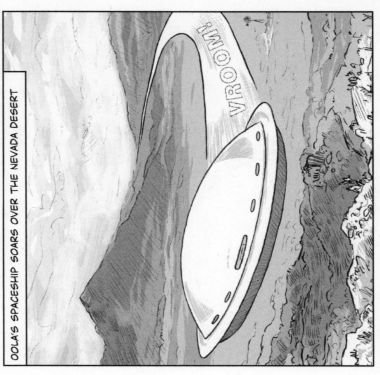

OOLA'S SPACESHIP SOARS OVER THE NEVADA DESERT

VROOM!

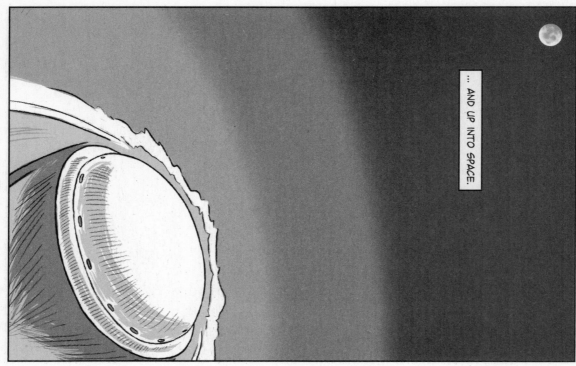

... AND UP INTO SPACE.

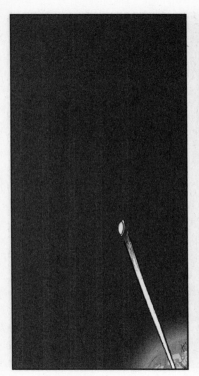

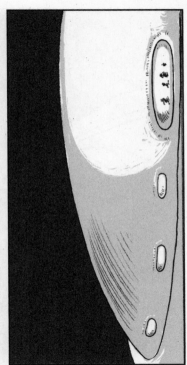

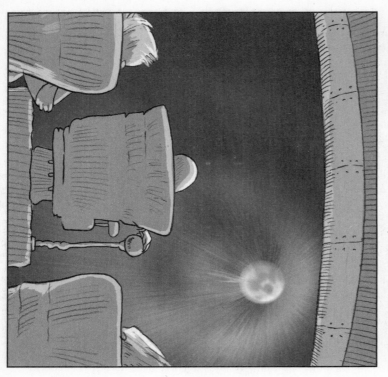

Albrecht scratched the fur around his neck. The suit was comfortable, but in the warm spaceship it was getting a little sticky.

"Oola," he said, peering at the walls of the ship, "who chose your wallpaper?"

The walls were decorated in weird and wonderful alien designs,

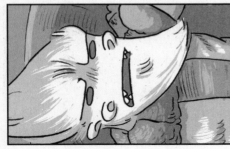

similar to the corridors. Some of the designs looked like Wiggly Fart Worms from the Triangulum Galaxy, while others resembled Globulous Pus Blobs from the outer arms of the Pinwheel Galaxy.

"These designs are classic Nargian prints," said Oola. "The finest in all the galaxy."

Albrecht was inclined to disagree, but he didn't want to offend.

"Do they come with matching lampshades?" he asked.

"In the rest rooms we have what you call 'carpets'," said Oola. "These are woven from the vomit of the Crangular Moth."

"Lovely," said Albrecht, wincing.

"So what brought you to Earth?" asked Saar.

"We had undertaken a tour of the galaxy," said Oola. "The Narg had travelled far, but Tala's energy was low. We hoped to find a power source on your planet."

"And did you?" asked Albrecht.

"No," said Oola. "Vuranium is not present on Earth."

"And why did you crash?" asked Saar.

"An electrical bolt knocked us from the sky," said Oola.

"I know how that feels," said Timonen. He looked at his fur and felt nostalgic for his old, brown-furred days.

"So if you were low on energy," asked Albrecht, "what's keeping us in the air now?"

"We still had enough Vuranium to fly two hundred light years," said Oola.

"I have no idea what that means," said Albrecht. The distances involved in space travel were enough to melt his brain.

"It's a long way," said Saar.

"Hey," said Timonen. "Where's this food, then?"

Oola walked to a machine nestled against the wall and switched it on.

"What would you like, oh furry one?" she said. "The Food Compositor can make you any meal you wish."

Timonen couldn't believe his luck.

"CURRY!" he shouted. "With peshwari naan and poppadum."

Oola typed the order into a small key panel.

"Have you ever thought about the toilet facilities of a space-suit?" asked Saar.

"What?" snapped Timonen. "Don't be ridiculous."

"Actually," asked Albrecht thoughtfully, "where are the toilets?"

"There are no toilets on board," said Oola. "The Narg expel toxins and waste through the skin."

"Ah," said Albrecht. "Good job I went before we left."

The Food Compositor pinged, and a plastic jar dropped into Oola's hand. It was full of blue, steaming liquid. She passed it to Timonen, who looked most confused. He sniffed the liquid.

"Smells like curry," he said.

He dunked his finger in it.

"Feels like curry," he said.

Then he downed the whole jar in one glug.

"Tastes like cardboard," he said. "URGH!"

Saar jumped to attention.

"I think I may cry with joy," he said. "The Moon is upon us."

The display was filled by the whole of the Moon's surface, its pale majesty so quiet and desolate.

"It is Ogragog," said Oola, rushing to her seat. "We have arrived."

She placed her hand on the terminal and piloted her ship. Boosters altered the ship's course and a large grey circular building, surrounded by three small domes, scrolled across the display. The buildings were nestled within the legions of craters that pockmarked the Moon's surface and were almost invisible but for faint turquoise lights that glowed around their edges.

"Is that the Moonbase?" asked Saar.

"Yes," said Oola, her huge eyes blinking. "But it is lit with emergency lights."

She sat quietly for a moment.

"I do not hear the Narg," she added.

"They're not there?" said Albrecht.

"Their voices are silent," said Oola.

The spaceship drew closer to the Moon's surface and Oola directed the craft to the Moonbase. A landing bay on the roof of the largest building was highlighted by faint concentric circles. Once the ship was in position, Oola initiated the landing procedure and metallic legs descended from the spaceship. With only a slight wobble it hit its mark.

Oola left her chair and patted the metal orb in thanks.

"We have reached Ogragog safely," she said, picking up her helmet. She slid it over her head and locked it in place. "Saviours of the Narg, it is time."

The yetis donned their helmets and followed Oola to the exit. Doors locked into place to create an airlock around them and, with everyone ready, the stairway folded out onto the Moonbase.

"We must proceed with caution," said Oola.

As the Moon's atmosphere replaced that on board the craft, Albrecht felt lightness in his feet. He bounced down the steps, breathing hesitantly while still cautious of his life-support apparatus. The bleak grey landscape of the Moon hit his eyes at the same time his feet hit the building, which shook beneath him in a way uncharacteristic of buildings. He thought nothing

more of it, his eyes entranced by the view.

The majestic peaks and plains of the Moon were devastated by impact craters. For millions of years, it had nobly defended the Earth from meteorites at the cost of its own beauty. And there at the edge of the horizon, was the Earth itself, radiant and seductive in the pure black sky.

Albrecht's sense of wonder was rudely smashed by an ominous roar below his feet.

"What was that?" said Albrecht, his voice relayed through everyone's helmet.

"What was what?" said Timonen. He jumped off the stairs and landed with a thump on the roof beside Albrecht. The roof shook, and a thin crack appeared beneath Albrecht's left foot.

"Stop!" he cried, as the crack lengthened, zigzagging across the roof. "It's not safe!"

Oola crept to the bottom of the steps and knelt down so she could place her hand on the Moonbase.

"Narg construction is stronger than this," she said, tapping her fingertips on the metal.

Timonen was about to walk away when Oola stopped him.

"Oh great furry one," she said, "do not move. Do not move even a muscle."

The crack widened between Albrecht's legs, stretching his feet a metre apart. He looked down into a chasm of darkness.

"Help," he pleaded, balancing himself, but the weight of the spaceship finally took its toll on the building.

"Hold tight!" shouted Saar as a large section of the roof imploded and the spaceship tilted forward. Timonen vanished deep into the building within a cloud of debris as three of the spaceship's metal legs lurched into the gaping hole. Oola and Saar were tossed forward helplessly and Albrecht was left dangling from a gnarled piece of metal. There was nothing but distant stars and moon dust to help him. He called to his friends but the silence was deafening.

Albrecht stretched higher with his right hand to find a firmer grip, but was left wanting. Below him was a swirling black cloud of impenetrable dust and his fingertips grew resigned to defeat.

"Hooray for low gravity," said Albrecht sourly, falling into the abyss.

"They say the best place to see stars is in space," said Saar, fruitlessly attempting to rub his aching head through his helmet. His eyes struggled to focus in the darkness, and the dim glow of his staff did little to light the area.

"Where is everyone?" he said.

"I'm here," said Timonen. "This place is as dark as a pile of yak dung."

"I'm somewhere," said Albrecht. "Is everyone okay? We must be pretty close to each other."

Suddenly two beams of light rippled through the dust. They were searchlights built into Oola's helmet.

"Do not move," said Oola calmly. "We are in a maintenance tunnel. I shall find you."

She beamed the lights around the area and eventually picked out the three yetis. They'd fallen through two floors of the building, coming to rest in a wide corridor scattered with debris.

"Those lights are handy," said Albrecht. The Moon's gravity made him feel lighter than air, and he stood up with ease.

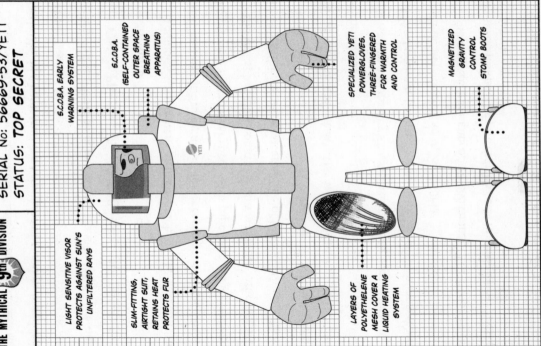

THE MYTHICAL **9th** DIVISION

ITEM: YETI SPACESUIT
SERIAL No: 5669-53/YETI
STATUS: *TOP SECRET*

LIGHT SENSITIVE VISOR
PROTECTS AGAINST SUN'S
UNFILTERED RAYS

SLIM-FITTING,
AIRTIGHT SUIT,
RETAINS HEAT
PROTECTS FUR

S.C.O.B.A. EARLY
WARNING SYSTEM

S.C.O.B.A.
(SELF-CONTAINED
OUTER SPACE
BREATHING
APPARATUS)

SPECIALIZED YETI
POWERGLOVES,
THREE-FINGERED
FOR WARMTH
AND CONTROL

MAGNETIZED
GRAVITY
CONTROL
STOMP BOOTS

LAYERS OF
POLYETHELENE
MESH COVER A
LIQUID HEATING
SYSTEM

"The Narg are good with design," said Oola.

"I guess that's why the roof collapsed," said Timonen sarcastically. He bounced across to Albrecht and bumped him off his feet.

"All life-support systems within the Moonbase are out," said Oola. "The auto-gravity facility has also failed. I am greatly worried."

Timonen's movement shifted much of the surrounding dust, making it briefly easier for everyone to see each other. The tunnel was tube-shaped, with pipes and cables strapped to the walls, but they could tell how weak the structure was. The metal walls were tattered like old lace, with crumbling, rusted sections eaten away throughout. A strange gloopy liquid was running down the walls, glistening in the glow of the lights.

"It's like a giant slug's been through here," said Albrecht.

"And it feels as though it's been deserted for years," added Saar.

"I do not understand it," said Oola.

She directed her lights down the tunnel.

"We must restore power," she said, running away. Each of

her steps was longer and lighter than they would have been on Earth.

Timonen was practising his high jumping, with his head nearly reaching the ceiling at the top of his jump.

"This is brilliant," he said, enjoying the low gravity.

"Stop mucking about," said Saar. He grabbed Timonen's feet mid-jump and pulled him down. "Your weight will make more of the building fall down."

"Even on the Moon you're tedious," said Timonen.

"Let's just get this over with," said Saar. "Then we can return to Earth in one piece."

"She's almost out of sight," said Albrecht, as the corridor fell dark once more. "Come on."

The three yetis raced after Oola.

"It's like Swiss cheese in here," said Saar, looking nervously around him at the holes in the walls.

"Whatever's going on," said Albrecht, "I don't like it."

They followed the tunnel round a bend and Oola slowed down.

"We have arrived," she said. "This is the power station."

She turned her head to illuminate a door that was hanging from its crumbling hinges.

"Don't get your hopes up," said Albrecht.

Oola stepped cautiously into the room. The circles of light from her helmet skipped over sections of machinery, much of which resembled that from Oola's ship.

"What can you see?" asked Saar.

Oola held out her hand, searching telepathically for some sign of life and then froze.

"What is it?" said Albrecht.

"Let me in," said Timonen. He barged past Albrecht and Saar and bounded in front of Oola. "What's in here, then?"

The lights from Oola's helmet were shining on an area at the far side of the room. Timonen leaped forward with little care.

"What's the matter?" he said. Then he realized.

Slumped on the floor next to a large metal sphere was an alien body. It was the last thing Timonen was expecting to see and he tripped and fell slowly to the floor. He scrambled back awkwardly.

"It is one of the Narg," said Oola, turning her lights away.

"I cannot look."

Saar nudged Timonen out of the way and entered the room.

The Staff of Ages was glowing brightly, warning of trouble.

Saar approached the Narg body and leant down to inspect it.

"Was he attacked?" asked Albrecht.

Saar looked closer. The alien was wearing a full spacesuit, but its helmet had been partially eaten away.

"I would guess he died from lack of oxygen," said Saar. "He seems unharmed, otherwise."

Saar ran his gloved finger across the helmet and found a film of the strange liquid that they'd seen on the walls of the corridor. It had formed a pool on the floor.

"I am sorry," said Saar to Oola.

"He suffered the same fate as our Moonbase," said Oola.

"How many others were here?" asked Albrecht.

"There were fifty-two," said Oola.

"Then dead or alive, they must be somewhere," said Albrecht.

"Can we get the generator working again?"

Oola aimed her lights at the metal sphere near the body and traced a route from its base to a unit on the wall.

"Let us try," she said.

She walked to the unit and pushed a lever up and down, before kicking it with force.

"It's good to see alien technology works the same as that of Earth," said Albrecht.

"The cables are broken beneath us," said Oola. "The generator will not start."

"Compromised, like everything else," said Saar.

"Even without power we need to start looking for your friends," said Albrecht.

"Where should we start?" asked Saar.

"I do not have an answer," said Oola. "If the Narg were here, I would hear their voices."

"Could they have left the base?" asked Albrecht.

"It is conceivable," said Oola.

"Do you have a map?" asked Saar.

"Not here," said Oola, "but there is one within Axrath in the observatory."

"Axrath?" asked Albrecht.

"The first great mistress of Ogragog!" said Oola. "But without power, we cannot access it."

Oola suddenly looked as though her world had fallen apart. She crouched to the ground clutching her chest.

"What's wrong?" asked Saar.

"With no power, the Narg will have had no air to breathe," she said.

Everyone sat quietly for a moment in the near darkness. It was silent until Albrecht's RoAR awoke on his backpack.

"Narg? Yetis? This is Grundy, over."

The voice made Albrecht jump. He pulled the RoAR from his pack and spoke to Grundy, whose face was already waiting for him on the screen.

"What have you found?" said Grundy.

"Nothing," said Albrecht. "It's deserted and falling apart."

"I wasn't expecting that," said Grundy. "The Narg are gone?"

"They've vanished," said Albrecht. "We're trying to find them right now."

"Do your best," said Grundy seriously. "It's imperative that you bring them home."

"Yes, sir," said Albrecht.

"I'll keep this channel open," said Grundy. "Inform me when

you're ready to return."

"I will," said Albrecht.

The RoAR's screen turned black and Albrecht returned it to the cradle on his backpack.

"So," said Saar to Oola. "Take us to this Axrath."

"We're resourceful," said Albrecht. "We might get lucky."

Oola stood upright.

"The Narg are lucky to have you," she said.

Chapter 5: The Search for Extraterrestrial Life

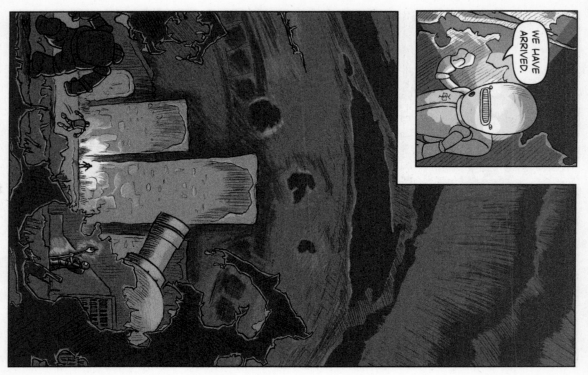

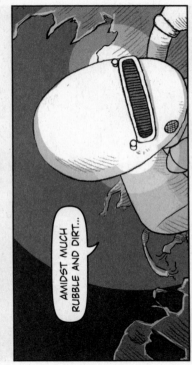

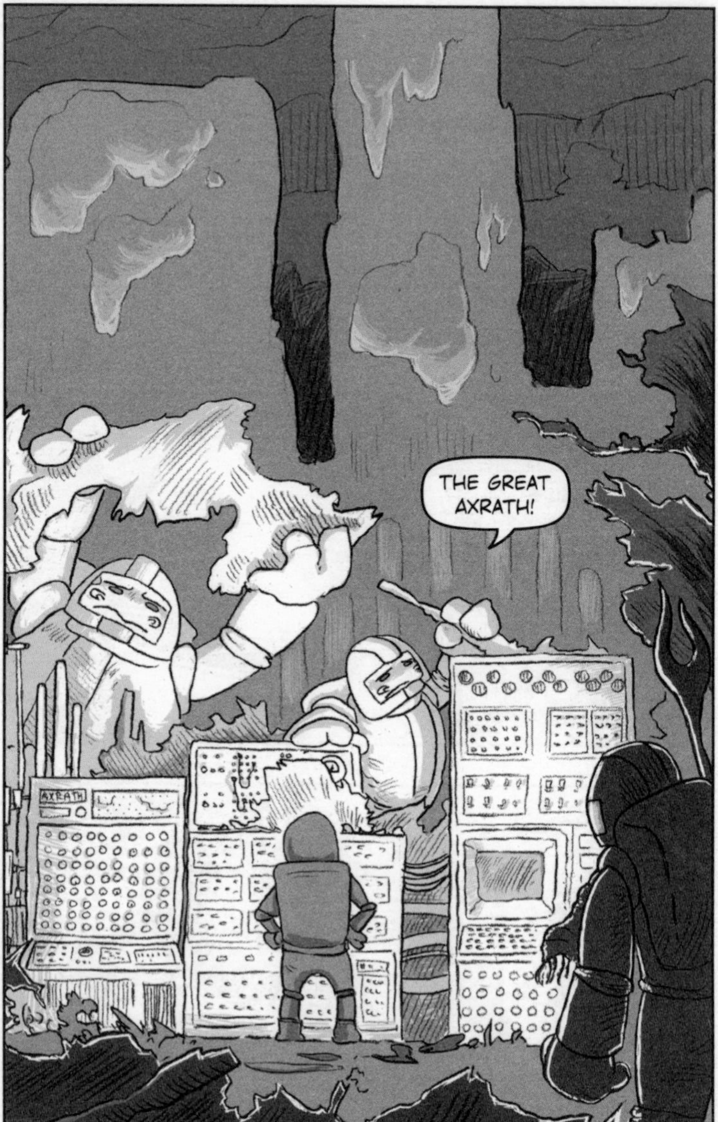
THE GREAT AXRATH!
AXRATH

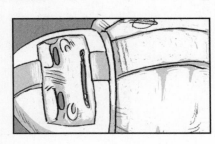

Albrecht retrieved the RoAR from his backpack and switched it on. Its startup screen was now black and showed the logo of the Mythical 7th Division, and its options appeared slightly different to usual. Most noticeable of all was the shortcut contact to Solomon Grundy on the homepage.

"Typical," said Albrecht. "Someone has a go on your device and it comes back all messed up."

"So what do you plan to do?" asked Saar.

"Axrath is a really old computer," said Albrecht. "The power in the RoAR's backup power cell should be more than enough to run it."

He removed the spare battery from the RoAR and pulled open part of the cabinet below the computer. There were thousands of wires, all bunched together in bundles. Paper labels were wrapped around them and Albrecht was soon in control of the situation.

"Right," he said, connecting up the battery. "Here goes nothing!"

A white line flickered onto the screen, and with a short burst of static, the words **NARG/NASA TECHNOLOGIES** appeared in bright white lettering.

"Now then," said Albrecht, reading himself at the keyboard.

He looked at the keys, but each button carried an unintelligible alien script instead of a letter.

"Ummm..." said Albrecht.

Oola asked to have a go, and Albrecht moved out of the way. Considering she only had three fingers, her typing was so fast as to be almost a blur. The screen flashed from a simple search engine to a complicated wire-frame schematic of the whole Moonbase.

"Bingo!" said Albrecht. "Now where is everyone?"

"I did not expect you to succeed," said Oola happily. "I may be able to access the station records."

"And?" said Timonen, who was thoroughly bored.

Oola almost burst with excitement. She bounced up and down. "I have them," she said. "The last entry..."

"What does it say?" asked Saar.

Oola read the statement aloud.

Moonbase Log, Stardate: 3.4433

Commander: Vringo of the Narg

Base infiltrated by invisible force. Mysterious clear liquid found in corridors. Structure seriously weakened and power lines failed. Airlocks breached and internal atmosphere contaminated. Narg evacuated and final recorded transmission sent to Earth. Life-force low. As remaining commander of Moonbase, I shall now attempt to revive the power generator to prevent total life-support system failure.

"Vringo of the Narg," said Oola, tearfully. "He never escaped."

Albrecht placed a hand on her shoulder.

"But he let us know that the rest of your people did," he said.

"They may still be alive."

"Oh, man," said Timonen restlessly. "What's the use of an invisible baddie?"

"It makes it very difficult for us to find it," said Saar.

"Exactly!" exclaimed Timonen. "This mission is rubbish! I want to smash something."

"Bring up the map," said Albrecht. "Where could they have gone?"

NARG LIVING POD INCLUDES: BED,
BRAIN CONNECTION FACILITY,
WASHSTATION AND RUG

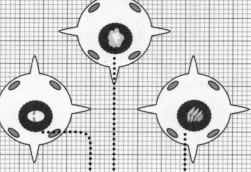

OUTPOST UNITS
INCLUDE: HYDROPONICS,
MINERAL RESOURCES
AND SPORTS

OUTPOST UNIT
TUNNELS

ITEM: MOONBASE*
SERIAL NO: 7001-99/NARG
STATUS: *TOP SECRET*

* TRANSLATED FROM THE
ORIGINAL NARGLISH

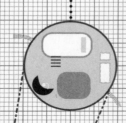

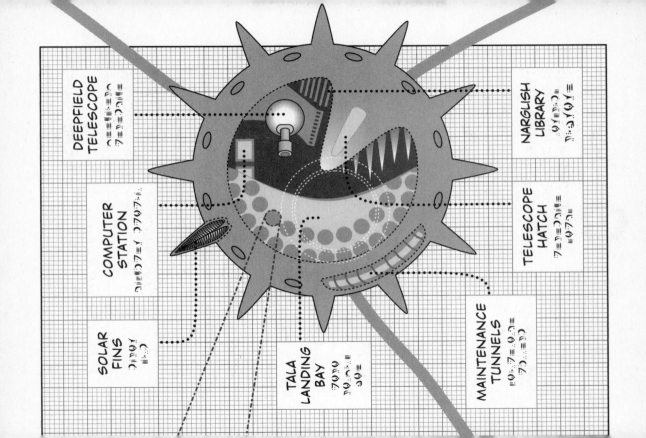

DEEPFIELD
TELESCOPE

NARGLISH
LIBRARY

COMPUTER
STATION

TELESCOPE
HATCH

SOLAR
FINS

TALA
LANDING
BAY

MAINTENANCE
TUNNELS

Oola returned to the base schematic and scanned the site. Albrecht pointed at the external domes that circled the main building.

"What are these?" he asked.

"Living quarters, workshops and mining resources," said Oola.

"Mining?" said Albrecht.

"The Narg have utilized a natural moon resource for fuel," said Oola. "The Moon is rich in Helium-3. We are hoping one day it will help us to get home."

"But a mine could be exactly what we're looking for," said Saar.

"Your brains are smaller, O furry saviours," said Oola, "but your minds are strong!"

Oola pointed to a beacon on the map, far outside the Moonbase. "The mine has a generator," said Oola. "The Narg are underground!"

A growl shook the air above them and a whole section of roof collapsed into the room sending a cloud of dust into the air. A cascade of goop covered Timonen from head to toe.

"What is this stuff?" he moaned. He flicked it from his arms and cleaned his helmet.

"It seems to follow the destruction," said Saar. "I'd pay it greater attention if it weren't for our lack of time and air."

"Speaking of that..." said Albrecht.

One of the walls fell in on itself, kicking up another plume of dust.

"We should leave before this place buries us alive," he said.

"Narg!" said Oola, "We are coming."

They ran at full speed through the Moonbase, eventually finding a massive opening in the crumbling wall that led out onto the Moon's surface. The light was a welcome change.

"What's that?" said Timonen, pointing off into the distance.

"They have cars on the Moon?"

"It's a moon buggy!" said Albrecht.

"You mean a lunar rover," said Saar.

"It was used in the final Ogragog mission," said Oola, struggling to keep up with the yetis, who were charging towards it. "The mission humans called Apollo 17."

"Does it still work?" asked Timonen, climbing in. The prospect of excitement was too much for him and he started randomly

pressing buttons with his thick-gloved fingers. Albrecht leaned over the chassis and looked at the controls.

"Try pushing that," he said, directing Timonen to a bar in between the seats.

Timonen pushed it and the buggy spluttered into life, its back wheels kicking up dust in great spurts. He skidded it around in a figure of eight, before stopping.

"Who wants a lift?" he said.

"Are you sure it can take the weight?" asked Saar. "I doubt it was designed for us."

"Who cares?" said Timonen. "It's not like we're ever coming back."

"It'll be quicker," said Albrecht getting on.

The others followed, and soon they were ploughing through the moon dust at a fairly reasonable 12 kilometres per hour.

"Towards the hill," said Oola.

In the shadow of a crater's edge, they pulled up to a metallic dome, a tiny version of those around the base. On its side was a set of heavy metal doors inscribed with alien lettering.

"This is it," said Albrecht.

He dropped down and bounced over to the doors.

"Sealed shut," said Albrecht, slamming his palms on the metal. "Timonen!"

"I can?" Timonen replied like an excitable puppy. He banged his fists together, knowing exactly what was required. "Out of the way, Albrecht."

With two extraordinary wallops, Timonen buckled the metal doors apart.

"There you go!" he said proudly.

The yetis and Oola stepped cautiously into the unlit tunnel. Oola's lights beamed from left to right as she walked with her hand raised high. They walked further and further downward, the only sound being that of their breath on their microphones. They passed mine carts and piles of rocks, and many abandoned lamps.

Oola stopped.

"What is it?" asked Albrecht.

She hesitated.

"Oola," said Saar, urgently. "What is it?"

Timonen strode to the front of the group and widened his

stance to fill the tunnel. He was very good at causing a blockage.

"I'll defend us," said Timonen. "Nothing can get past me."

Oola lowered her hand.

"The Narg are alive!" she cried.

Timonen's shape was lit momentarily as a black silhouette. Beams of light hit him like a wall of floodlights on a football pitch.

"Woah!" shouted Timonen, blinking, as fifty aliens squeezed past him, chattering incessantly and triumphantly. It was the sound of a civilization being saved. Oola was so overjoyed that she jumped up and down. The rest of the Narg were also bouncing for joy.

"That was easy enough," said Albrecht.

"Let's not speak too soon," declared Saar. "We still need to get out of here."

The aliens had surrounded the yetis and were clutching them like lost friends. Timonen lifted four Narg onto his shoulders.

"They're calling me the Mighty Fluff," he said proudly.

"That sounds about right," said Saar.

Oola called for quiet.

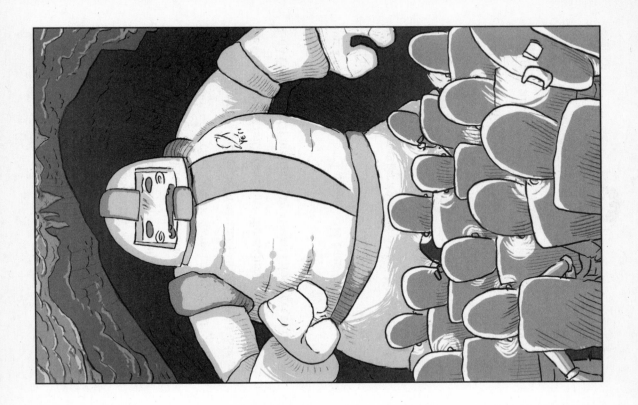

"O great furry ones," she said. "My fellow Narg have told me things."

"And?" said Albrecht.

"The invisible foe favours metal," said Oola. "The Narg have heard him eating. Our craft is in serious danger."

The threat stirred Albrecht into action.

"How many of us can fit on the moon buggy?" said Albrecht.

"Not enough," said Saar. "You and Oola go ahead. Me and the Mighty Fluff will make sure these aliens get to safety."

"What?!" said Timonen. "You mean I don't get to drive the buggy?"

"That's exactly what I mean," said Saar. "It's for the greater good."

Timonen threw another two aliens onto his shoulders.

"Fine," he said grumpily. "Come with me, you little Nargies."

Chapter 6: Meeting with the Enemy

ALBRECHT AND OOLA SET OFF IN THE MOON BUGGY. TIME IS RUNNING OUT

The crumbling walls of the Moon-base were falling apart about them.

"We've got a job on our hands here," said Albrecht.

"Tala's trapped amongst debris," said Oola.

"Then we'll have to help her out," said Albrecht.

He made his way to the curving wall and climbed up under the glow of one of the blue emergency lights. The mysterious goop was seeping from every hole that served as a delicate footing for Albrecht.

"Watch yourself!" he said to Oola, who was finding the climb difficult. Her hands couldn't reach the same holes as Albrecht's, but she laboured on to a point two thirds of the way up, where Albrecht had stopped to survey the way forward.

"These are Narg sleeping quarters," said Oola, pointing out the hexagonal sleeping bays now exposed to the Moon's atmosphere.

"You'd have a nice view of the stars from those beds," said Albrecht.

"A Narg would prefer a roof," said Oola.

The walls continued to crumble about them and their very footing became unsure.

"I don't want to hang around," said Albrecht. "Which way now?"

"The landing pad is central," said Oola. "We can head inwards."

Suddenly, Saar's voice crackled into Albrecht's earpiece.

"I don't want to alarm you," he said, "but the lights in my helmet have turned red."

Albrecht looked about inside his helmet. His lights were definitely still blue.

"And Timonen's?" asked Albrecht.

Timonen's voice blathered into Albrecht's helmet.

"His special yeti powers are eating all his air," he said. "I'm still blue."

"I think we should hurry," said Saar.

"Oh..." said Timonen, mumbling.

"What," said Albrecht.

"I've gone red, too," he replied. "That wasn't supposed to happen."

"Your air is running out six hours ahead of schedule," said Albrecht. "This isn't right!"

"Should I stop breathing?" asked Timonen.

"And put us all out of our misery?" asked Saar. "Yes, please."

"Right," said Albrecht. "Don't move another muscle. The more you exert yourself, the more oxygen you use up."

"So I can have a lie down?" asked Timonen.

"On this occasion," said Albrecht, "it may save your life."

"Awesome," said Timonen.

Oola pointed into the Moonbase.

"We must enter," she said.

"Okay," said Albrecht. "You guys stay put. We're coming to get you."

"Hurry," said Saar, "I can already sense the air thinning."

"Then stop talking!" said Albrecht. "Don't waste a breath."

Oola rushed through the alien quarters, the floor threatening to give way at every step. Albrecht took giant steps to lighten the load on the metal below him, and they soon reached the heart of the base. Heavy iron girders crashed around them, revealing rooms which quickly tumbled through the floor to oblivion.

"There!" said Oola. She pointed to a narrow disc of metal cutting through a section of crumpled roof. "My ship!"

"And she's still in one piece!" said Albrecht.

They ran on, dodging the falling building's attempts to flatten them. When they reached the spaceship, they realized she was so precariously balanced that one foot in the wrong place could spell disaster. A heavy roof section was resting on its top.

"You go ahead, Oola," said Albrecht. "You're lighter than me."

The floor creaked as Oola lifted a small section of crumpled panelling to reveal the open staircase into the spaceship. It was now near vertical and unusable.

"I need your assistance," said Oola, stretching up. "You'll have to throw me in."

"I can do that," said Albrecht.

He shuffled along the edge of what was left of the corridor and took a strong hold of Oola. She weighed next to nothing.

"Get ready," said Albrecht.

With all his strength, he tossed Oola high into the craft.

As she gripped the edge of the spaceship, Albrecht's feet burst through the floor. Thinking quickly he grabbed one of the spaceship's metal legs.

"Don't panic!" he shouted, as the whole floor broke up and smashed into the ground. "I'm all right!"

The spaceship was left wobbling on a stretch of wall. It was no longer trapped, but looked ready to drop. Oola pulled herself inside and peeked over the edge at Albrecht.

"Hold on!" she said. "Tala will save you!"

Oola raced into her craft and closed the staircase. The spaceship rocked with her added weight.

"Beautiful Tala," she said. "Fire retro-boosters."

Outside, Albrecht watched in horror as six boosters roared into action. White heat fired out of the underside of the craft in cylindrical bursts, narrowly missing him.

"Save me?!" shouted Albrecht, his body getting blown left and right. "You're gonna burn me alive!"

"Tala," said Oola, her hand pressed to the terminal near her chair in the control room, "cease boosters and increase forward thrusters."

The boosters stopped and Albrecht had time to breathe a misplaced sigh of relief before the spaceship dropped a few metres lower, jarring his wrists and almost causing him to let go.

"What are you doing!" he cried, as he pulled himself up the metal leg and wrapped his feet around its base for safety.

The spaceship screamed as thrusters dislodged it from the wall and sent it rocketing upwards just in time. Unable to cope with the force of the take-off, the walls of the Moonbase twisted and toppled to the ground.

Albrecht squeezed his eyes shut.

"Put me down!" he cried.

With a lightness of touch so far missing from its escape, the spaceship drifted to a very gentle stop just metres from the rescued Narg.

Albrecht slid from the leg and collapsed to the ground.

The Narg cheered.

Saar's air levels had diminished to the point that he was struggling to breathe, but he found his feet. The spaceship's door opened up, and Oola hurried everyone inside. Timonen picked

up Albrecht from the floor and took him in.

Once Oola had sealed the ship, Saar removed his helmet and breathed deeply. At that moment, he noticed his right glove had small holes littering its surface.

"Timonen," said Saar, frowning. "Do you have these?"

"What?" said Timonen, unclasping his helmet. As he did so, the metal seal around his neck crumbled to dust in his hands.

"That might answer our lack of air," said Saar. "Take a look at this, Albrecht."

The three yetis stared at Timonen's helmet. It was turning to ribbons before their eyes. His suit was also covered with small holes, like Saar's glove.

"Let the Narg see," said Oola.

She ran her eyes over Timonen's space-suit and asked him to lift up his arm. There were more holes in his armpit, and some of the strange goop from the Moonbase remained in its folds.

"I don't like this strange liquid," said Saar.

"Tala," said Oola. "Open the laboratory."

A large section of wall dropped down, revealing a surgical workbench lined with tools. Oola retrieved a clear glass dish, scooped some of the liquid into it and placed it under a microscope. The image of the liquid magnified a thousand times was shown on the main viewing screen.

"I've never seen anything like it," said Saar.

"Our invisible foe is now anything but invisible," said Oola. "It is a new species of Nanogrime."

"Nano-what?" said Timonen.

The image on the screen was of something far more sinister than mere slime. Hundreds of horrific microscopic creatures,

formed almost entirely of teeth, were bustling about like popping corn. Oola performed a more detailed scan of the liquid.

"They are composed of many metals," she said.

"And they're multiplying," said Albrecht.

The tiny creatures kept splitting in two before their eyes.

The goop was growing in size in the dish.

"We need to get them out of the ship," said Saar, removing his spacesuit at breakneck speed and trying to whip Timonen into some sort of fervour. "If this stuff gets loose in here, we won't make it home."

"Oola," said Albrecht. "We must act fast."

"But my ship," said Oola. "She is covered in it already."

"Then we have even less time," said Saar. "You've seen how quickly it ate through our suits. We must head for Earth immediately before it takes hold on the ship."

"You are right," said Oola. "Narg! We must eject our suits."

The many Narg swept up everyone's spacesuits and jettisoned them from the craft. They then scoured the decks to ensure none of the Nanogrime remained.

Oola placed her hand on the terminal and prepared to escape.

"STOP!" cried Albrecht.

Their true predicament had finally hit home.

"But we can't go anywhere," he said.

"What?" said Timonen. "Don't be an idiot."

Albrecht shook his head.

"We can't risk this stuff landing on Earth!" he said. "It could be the end of civilization as we know it."

"Flaming yaks," said Saar. "You're right. We can't ever go home."

"But there's no food here," said Timonen. "Just cardboard-flavoured juice!"

"Of all the times to think of that," said Albrecht. "I'll contact Grundy."

He grabbed his RoAR and booted it up. He hit the contact button for Grundy, and in seconds his face was on the screen.

"What is it?" said Solomon Grundy. "Is there a problem?"

"We have the Narg," said Albrecht. "But time is short. I want an immediate answer."

"Fire away," said Grundy.

"Our ship's been compromised by a metal-eating Nanogrime," said Albrecht.

"A Nano-form?" said Grundy excitedly. "We've not encountered one of those for almost fifteen years."

"So you know of this stuff?" said Albrecht.

"We have benign samples in containment," said Grundy. "But nothing that powerful."

"I fear we cannot risk returning to Earth," said Albrecht. "If this Nanogrime gets loose it could destroy everything."

"Let's not jump to conclusions," said Grundy. "How compromised are you?"

"We think it's currently only on the outer shell," said Albrecht.

"Then there is a chance," said Grundy. "Our planet has an amazing defence mechanism in its atmosphere. Without protection, very little will survive the heat of re-entry."

"A valid point," said Saar. "But one that also applies to our spacecraft."

"Narg technology is stronger than you imagine," said Grundy. "Besides, if you stay there, the Nanogrime will eat through your craft, giving you no chance of survival. You have to risk returning to Earth."

"The odds are against us," said Albrecht.

THE MYTHICAL 9TH DIVISION   124   The Alien Moon

"They are," said Grundy, "but LEGENDS cannot lose both the Narg and the Mythical 9th Division so easily. You must return."

"You heard the man!" said Timonen.

"Is that your order?" asked Albrecht.

"That's my order," said Grundy. "I'll place the rescue teams on standby."

Albrecht switched off the RoAR, strapped on his regulation backpack and locked the straps.

"Oola, fire up the engines," he said. "We're going home."

Sirens wailed over Area 51, and Compound W was a hive of hurried activity. Grundy's DECON had been put under red alert.

"Ready our attack force," ordered Solomon Grundy, marching along a yellow-painted walkway. "And arm our troops with Electrobolts. These yetis are meddlesome and capable of trouble."

"Yes, sir," said a soldier. "The other mythical divisions are now well on their way home."

"Our efficiency does us proud," said Grundy.

"We did have a problem removing the goblins from the base," added the soldier, "but that's been dealt with now."

"I should hope so," said Grundy. "We don't have time for diversions."

"No, sir," said the soldier.

Engines revved around the base, and Solomon Grundy leaped into the passenger seat of an armour-plated jeep. He took hold of the Mythical 7th Division badge that was sewn onto his suit jacket. With a sharp tear, the front piece of cloth tore off to reveal a tattered alien skull and the word DECON. There was no need to hide his true self any more.

"To the desert," said Grundy. "And world domination."

Chapter 7: Return of the Yeti

Bright red flames rippled from the edges of the spaceship as it hit the Earth's atmosphere. Heat was building on its surface, eating into the weakened sections of the craft.

Oola hadn't moved from the metal orb, despite the craft shaking violently through turbulence.

"Tala's suffering," she said.

"And it's warming up in here," said Albrecht.

"Tell me about it," said Timonen.

He was covered in Narg, who felt protected within the reach of his arms.

"That's what comes from being the Mighty Fluff," said Saar.

He was clutching his staff tight and had his arm locked around Oola's chair.

Everything inside the craft was rattling loudly, and the noise grew to a deafening pitch.

"If we make it through re-entry," shouted Albrecht, "will we be able to land?"

"Tala will look after us," said Oola.

Panels within the ship popped from the walls. Glass cases cracked. Wallpaper peeled off.

"She can't take much more of this," said Saar.

"Tala be strong," willed Oola. "Tala be strong."

As quickly as it had started, the bright fire surrounding the craft died away and was replaced with silence. The spaceship was hurtling through the lower reaches of the atmosphere.

"We're through," said Saar, his grip loosening.

"What's the damage?" said Albrecht.

Oola communicated with her ship.

"Landing gear destroyed," said Oola. "Communications down and forward thrusters depleted."

"Doesn't sound too bad," said Timonen.

"Apart from the fact that we won't be able to land," said Saar.

"Where are we aiming for?" said Albrecht.

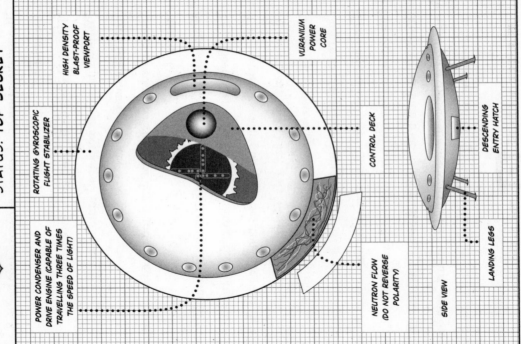

THE MYTHICAL 9th DIVISION

ITEM: NARG SPACECRAFT (TALA)
SERIAL No: 7002-87/NARG
STATUS: TOP SECRET

HIGH DENSITY BLAST-PROOF VIEWPORT

VURANIUM POWER CORE

ROTATING GYROSCOPIC FLIGHT STABILIZER

CONTROL DECK

POWER CONDENSER AND DRIVE ENGINE (CAPABLE OF TRAVELLING THREE TIMES THE SPEED OF LIGHT)

NEUTRON FLOW (DO NOT REVERSE POLARITY)

DESCENDING ENTRY HATCH

SIDE VIEW

LANDING LEGS

"Tala is targeting the site of launch," said Oola. "But her voice is faint. I cannot hear her clear thoughts."

"So no news about the Nanogrime?" asked Saar.

"I cannot tell," replied Oola.

"How long until we hit ground," said Albrecht.

"Without Tala, I do not know," said Oola.

"Best brace ourselves then," said Saar.

Oola rushed to her chair, sat down and placed her hand on the terminal.

"Fire boosters," she said, operating the craft manually.

The boosters spat white-hot fire from the bottom of the craft, momentarily slowing down its descent. Then they failed.

"Boosters out," said Oola. "Tala, please…"

"I might just close my eyes really tight," said Albrecht.

"You're so brave," said Timonen.

The Earth filled the viewing panel. They passed over Africa and the Atlantic Ocean, clouds whizzing above and below them like giant, never-ending white sheets. America was soon filling the screen, a massive jumble of greens and browns, greys and blues. Mountains and rivers blurred into each other, passing by at lightning fast speed. Each second was taking them lower to the ground.

"We are travelling too fast!" said Oola, attempting to rouse Tala's systems. She jumped to her feet and held the orb with both hands.

"Invert gravity system," said Oola.

With the desert filling the screen, the yetis and Narg lifted into the air on a wave of invisible force.

"Impact imminent..." said Oola.

Albrecht glanced at the screen and witnessed impending doom. He tried to think of something important to say, but all that came out was a terrified "RAAAAAAR!"

The spaceship crashed into the ground with the force of a speeding bullet. Lumps of rock and dirt sprayed high into the air and a thick tower of black smoke belched into the sky.

A circle of vultures formed above the crash site, their shadows mixing with the crash debris and fires burning on the desert floor.

"I think I'm still alive," said Albrecht, who was surprised to find the floor was upright.

The gravity machine in the craft had created a safety barrier, cushioning everyone inside as it crashed. There was no light, and the air was thick with smoke, but the cheers of the jubilant Narg brightened the situation.

"And you aliens survived, too," he added.

"Tala saved us," said Oola, crawling across a metal unit. "O great furry saviours, you have brought us to safety!"

"Second time in a day that I've got a headache," said Saar.

"And Timonen?" said Albrecht. "Where are you?"

"Don't worry about me," he said. "The Nargies softened the landing."

Timonen was lying on a stretch of wall, which now doubled up as the floor.

"We need to get out," said Albrecht. "This smoke will kill us." Saar's staff was glowing blue and provided a small amount of light. It was enough to see by and he pointed to where he remembered the door to be. It wasn't there any more.

"Wait there," said Timonen.

He stood up and pulled at a section of what used to be the floor. It fell apart in his hands and a chink of smoky light burst in. It was very obvious that although the deck of the spaceship was intact, the rest of it hadn't fared anything like as well.

"Not very thick these walls, are they?" he said.

Oola scrambled over to him to get a better look.

"Tala!" she cried. "There's nothing of you!"

Timonen punched through more of the wall and as he did more light flooded in. All that remained of the craft was the

central control deck, now just a blackened box in a thick dome of smoke.

"It's hot out there!" said Timonen.

"Unsurprising considering the crash," said Saar. He stepped over and looked out into the wall of impenetrable smoke. "We'll have to run for it."

"I'm with you," said Albrecht. "Somewhere out there lies safety."

"We shall follow," said Oola. "But first, I must pay my respects."

Oola reached to the metal orb and touched it with her fingertips. There was still life inside, but the voice she knew as Tala was now less than a whisper.

"Goodbye, my friend," she said. She lowered her hand in a gesture that told Albrecht she was ready.

"Right," said Albrecht. "Hold your breath!"

They broke through the ship's wall and entered the dense smoke in a blaze of glory. The blast crater beneath their feet was still scorching from the crash. Each step was more like a hop to avoid suffering the heat on the soles of their feet. The smoke seemed to go on forever, stinging their eyes.

Finally, with a *whoosh* of fresh air against their faces, they

reached safety. Albrecht opened his eyes and wasted no time in collapsing on the ground, coughing heavily. The cracked floor of the desert felt like an oasis to his body.

"Hello, planet," he said, kissing the dusty, parched floor. Surrounded by friends and aliens, Albrecht looked back at the crash site. There was so much smoke it was impossible to see anything of Tala.

"Did we really survive that?" said Albrecht.

"The yeti gods have been kind," said Saar.

"Have we landed on the sun?" asked Timonen, his tongue lolling out of his mouth. He was sweating buckets through his thick shaggy fur. The Narg followed him around as though he was their leader.

"It's hotter than ever out here," he whined.

"You have a point," said Saar. "Where's a tree when you need one?"

"Just for this moment," said Albrecht peacefully. "I don't care how hot it is, I want to lie here."

He had never considered how much he really loved his planet until now.

"Speaking of shade," said Saar, who was tending to his charred feet. "What just blocked the sun?"

The whole of the area was cast in shadow.

"Oh great furry ones," said Oola, running to Albrecht in panic. "We are not alone."

Chapter 8: The Secrets of Solomon

143

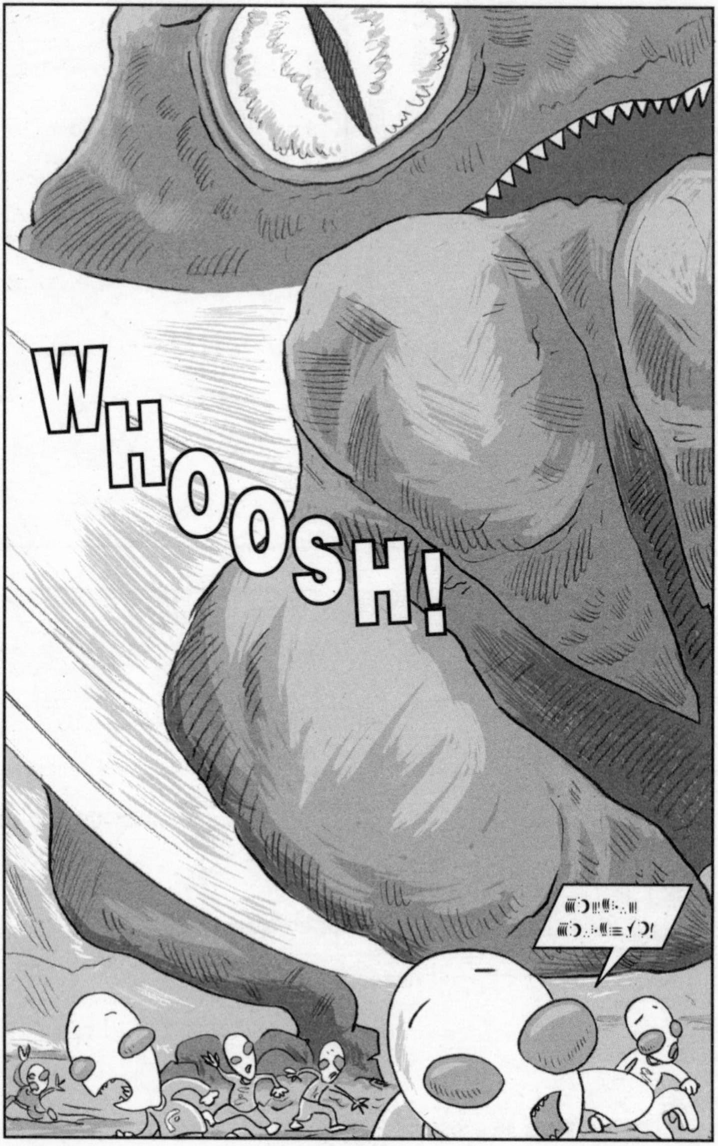
WHOOSH!

To describe the monster as horrible would be doing a disservice to horrible things. Its four gangly arms and two gangly legs held up its enormous body like twigs supporting a fully grown oak tree. Its head was a glistening, rounded lump atop its shoulders and there must have been nearly a million

teeth in its mouth, not to mention its two giant, fiery eyes.

The monster roared again, but didn't follow the yetis and aliens. It delved inside the tower of smoke and reappeared with the remains of the spaceship in its hand.

"Tala!" cried Oola, as her short legs carried her out across the desert. She stopped and watched as the massive monster devoured the heart of her spaceship.

"What are you thinking?" boomed Timonen, picking her up and flinging her onto his shoulder.

"Wait!" said Albrecht. "It's not chasing us. Look!"

The monster stepped out of the smoke and started sniffing the air. Drool cascaded onto the desert. Once it had caught a

scent, it stomped off into the distance, making short work of the hills. The ground shook with each pounding blow.

"What's it doing?" said Saar.

"It has eaten Tala," said Oola, from the unusually high position of Timonen's back.

"Hang on," said Albrecht. "The monster eats metal?"

"And suffers from prolific drooling?" said Saar.

"The Nanogrime..." said Albrecht. He was hit by a catastrophic thought. "We hoped to kill it by entering the atmosphere..."

"But instead we appear to have transformed it," said Saar, "and created a goop-making mega monster."

Albrecht returned to the crash site and found a pool of drool.

"It looks the same," he said wearily, surveying it from all angles.

"Put me down!" said Oola, tapping Timonen on the back. She rubbed her large forehead, and conversed with the Narg.

"We have heard of creatures like this," she said. "Species that cross galaxies."

"But how could the Nanogrime travel?" asked Albrecht.

"It's just slime."

"The Narg retrieved a meteorite from the Moon's surface,

shortly before I lost contact. The Nanogrime must have come with it."

"Travelled through space on a rock?" said Timonen.

"Exactly so," said Oola. "But unlike the Moon, where there is little atmosphere, entry into the Earth's atmosphere provided it with enough heat to grow up."

"The heat transformed it?" asked Albrecht.

"That is our theory," said Oola. "And we Narg are rarely wrong on these matters."

Saar was impressed.

"Quite brilliant," said Albrecht. "In the worst possible way."

"But you know what this means," said Saar.

"The monster's hungry," said Albrecht.

"Just like me!" said Timonen, but everyone ignored him.

"What's the closest source of metal?" asked Saar.

Albrecht switched on his RoAR and checked their location on a satellite map.

"There's not much but desert and mountains for miles," he said.

"That's a relief," said Saar.

"Ah," mumbled Albrecht, re-evaluating his last statement.

"Have any of you heard of Las Vegas?"

Saar banged his staff against his head.

"How do we get ourselves into these positions," he said.

"LAS VEGAS!" shouted Timonen excitedly. "Bring on the money!"

Albrecht tried to hide his exasperation, but it was next to impossible under the circumstances.

"I'd best contact Grundy," he said.

It took the RoAR mere seconds to find a connection and for Solomon Grundy's face to appear on the screen. He was in a moving vehicle, and his head bounced about the screen.

"We've already triangulated your position," said Grundy.

"We're heading your way. How are the Narg?"

"Their ship is destroyed," said Albrecht, "but they appear to be in one piece."

"Good," said Grundy. "The crash site is now under surveillance. No one gets in and no one gets out without me knowing. Any sign of the Nanogrime?"

"Sadly, yes," said Albrecht.

"Keep your distance," said Grundy. "We can handle it."

Albrecht coughed.

"But there's also a giant space monster heading towards Las Vegas," he added meekly. "It's spitting the Nanogrime all over the place."

Grundy made some hand signals to people behind him in the vehicle.

"That's unexpected," said Grundy, his one eye stretching open wide. "How big is it?"

"Sort of massive," said Albrecht.

Grundy looked away from the screen, receiving new information from a soldier.

"Okay," he said, turning back, "I have it on visual. We'll block phone signals and jam outgoing transmissions. I'll order an evacuation immediately."

"We think the monster was originally some of the Nanogrime," said Albrecht. "Re-entry into Earth's atmosphere had an effect on it."

"If that's true it would be extraordinary," said Grundy. He squeezed his chin with his thumb and forefinger. "However, I have no doubt I can get it under control."

"Phew!" said Albrecht, relieved.

"It's time," said Grundy. "I'm within sight of you. Signing off." Albrecht put the RoAR into his backpack and looked out across the desert. Lines of dust puffed into the air at the edge of the mountains; the trails of numerous armoured jeeps and vehicles.

"What are they?" said Saar.

"Grundy and the rescue team," said Albrecht, relieved.

"They look more like a tank regiment," said Timonen.

"They've even got rocket launchers."

The vehicles closed in, circling the Narg and the yetis. Grundy's cyborg soldiers bounded out of the vehicles and surrounded them.

"Why the funny outfits?" said Timonen.

The troops raised their Electrobolt weapons and aimed them at the yetis.

"Yeah, hi," said Albrecht. "Why the guns?"

The soldiers marched closer, and one approached Albrecht.

"You're all to come with us," said the soldier.

"I don't follow," said Albrecht, standing tall.

"Explain yourselves," snarled Saar.

"You have been exposed to lethal anti-human biology," said

the soldier. "You are now in the custody of DECON."

Albrecht was furious. Timonen was frothing at the mouth.

"Are they threatening us?" he said, cracking his knuckles.

He lowered the Narg and moved towards the soldiers.

"I would reassess your actions," said the soldier.

"Where is Grundy?" said Albrecht. "I want to speak with him."

"Our Captain does not want to be contaminated," said the soldier.

"I'll contaminate him," growled Timonen, "with my fists!"

"Threat level raised," said the soldier. "Employ the stunners."

Three soldiers unleashed an electrified web over the yetis, its crackling power toppling all three, before easing. The soldiers rushed around and secured them before they could move.

"What was that?!" cried Saar. Shivers and ticks rippled down his limbs.

"We have weapons to bring down any foe," said the soldier.

He looked at his men and spoke again. "Prepare the cargo for transportation!"

"Cargo?" said Saar, wrapped in the web and lying on the floor. "This isn't how I imagined we'd be greeted."

"If only I could contact Ponkerton," said Albrecht, struggling against his bonds. "This must be some sort of mistake."

The soldiers forced the yetis to their feet and led them and the Narg to an armoured vehicle.

"Furry saviours, do not worry," said Oola, joining alongside them. "The Narg are strong!"

They were all prodded into the back of the metal container and just before the doors could close, Grundy appeared outside.

"You did well," he said, keeping his distance.

Albrecht growled angrily.

"What are you up to?" he said.

Grundy held up a glass specimen jar filled with Nanogrime.

"The Nanogrime I was expecting," he said. "But the monster? Well, that's just the icing on the cake."

"You've gone to the dark side?" said Saar.

Grundy scratched his eyebrow. His eye patch shifted slightly, revealing a glimpse of metal below.

"I'm simply making the most of the situation," he said. "Imagine a warhead armed with a simple canister of this goop. Imagine one fired at every major city in the world. Before long, humanity will be on its knees and under my control."

"You don't know what that liquid's capable of!" growled Saar.

"Clearly I do," said Grundy. "I've been watching you from secret surveillance satellites. I saw the Moonbase disintegrate with my own eyes. I hadn't expected so many of you to survive the return trip, but there we go."

"You've gone mad," said Albrecht.

"I've finally found my true calling," he said.

"But the Mythical Divisions are supposed to protect Earth!" pleaded Albrecht.

"A sadly depressing notion," said Grundy. "Humans should command and conquer, not compromise!"

"You are wrong," said Saar.

"Once I've captured the monster and restrained it, I'll reveal my plans to the world. You've seen the arsenal at Compound W. We're unstoppable."

"You are no longer a friend of the Narg," said Oola.

"Ah," said Grundy, "but we've learned all there is to know of your species. And without your craft you are nothing."

"You won't get away with this," said Albrecht. "Not with us around."

"You won't be around," said Grundy. "You're contaminated goods and, as such, will need indefinite containment."

"Woah!" said Albrecht, "Hang on a minute."

"There is a quarantine cell a mile below Compound W that will be perfect for you."

"Ponkerton won't let this happen," said Albrecht.

"That old fool?" said Grundy.

"Take that back!" said Albrecht defensively.

"Where is he now, then?" said Grundy. "Only an idiot would let his operatives vanish from sight."

"He's no idiot," said Albrecht.

"Believe that if you wish," said Grundy. "But now, we

must part ways."

He smiled venomously and slammed the doors shut. Bolts clanked together, locking it tight.

"When I get out of here," said Timonen, "I'm going to throw that Grundy right back to the Moon."

"And I'll help you," said Albrecht.

"As one, we are strong," said Oola.

The aliens repeated her words in chorus.

"Something will turn up," said Saar.

"The end of the world?" said Albrecht.

He growled as the engines fired and the truck sped off.

The route had been bumpy and uncomfortable.

"I'm going to starve in precisely three minutes," said Timonen.

He felt as though his stomach was imploding.

"You'd better get used to being hungry," said Saar. "It'll be prison gruel from now on."

"I won't go hungry," said Timonen, restlessly trying to free his arms. "I'd eat you lot before I starve."

"At least we know where we stand," said Albrecht.

Suddenly the truck juddered and swerved. The engine cut out and they stopped moving.

"What is it?" said Albrecht.

Saar pressed his ears to the metal walls.

"I can hear…" said Saar. He looked confused. "It sounds like someone, no, lots of people, chewing."

Albrecht and Timonen also pressed their ears to the walls.

"Sounds like a massive tin opener at work," said Albrecht.

With a creak and a crunch, a small hole opened in the roof of the truck and a shard of light cut through. Gradually, a zigzag line appeared around the thick metal ceiling and, like a sardine tin lid, rolled back to reveal the open sky. A line of small green heads, with pointy ears and darkened goggles, popped up over the sides of the truck.

"YETIS!" shouted the goblins. "It's time to PARTAY!"

They threw themselves into the truck and chewed through the bindings on the yetis' hands.

"Good afternoon, furries," said Grizzle, the head goblin. He pulled proudly at the straps on his thin backpack. "We are the rescue team."

"When did we call for a rescue team?" said Saar.

"We didn't," said Albrecht.

"We're being resuced by goblins?" said Timonen. "Annoying little goblins?"

The goblins burst into laughter.

"The big yeti is funnier than we remembered," said Grizzle.

"What are these little things?" He was pointing at the Narg, who were shuffling about awkwardly in the cramped space. They were slightly taller than the goblins, but that didn't seem apparent to Grizzle.

"These *little things* are the noble race of the Narg," said Albrecht.

"The Narg?!" said Grizzle, squeaking a little. He burst into laughter, and the other Goblins copied him instantly. "What sort of a name is that?!"

Oola raised her hand and fine-tuned Grizzle's brain so that they could understand each other. Grizzle's eyes popped and swirled and he clenched his ears to stop them from hurting. The intense pain quickly subsided.

"The Narg are grateful for your kindness," said Oola. "Please

repeat what you said."

Grizzle's thoughts slipped by with the consistency of min-estrone soup.

"I said I was pleased to help," he replied, snarling a little.

"How did you know where we were?" said Albrecht, stretching out his fingers and rubbing his free wrists.

"Captain Ponkerton sent us," he replied. "You furries have homing devices."

"Like pet dogs," said another goblin.

"WOOF! WOOF!" screamed two goblins excitedly, who looked as if they might wet themselves at any moment.

"I'd forgotten about those," said Albrecht.

"I, for one, am grateful," said Saar.

Grizzle rammed his fist into his mouth to stop himself from laughing at the mystical yeti.

"What's so funny?" asked Saar.

"I'm so grateful!" squealed a goblin, mockingly.

"I'm so grateful, too!" said another.

"This is going to tire very quickly," said Saar. "We've been rescued by a team of pre-schoolers."

The goblins laughed again.

"I need to contact Ponkerton," said Albrecht, shaking his head. Grizzle wiped the tears from his eyes.

"This way!" he said. "We have goblin phones in the goblinmobile."

The back doors of the truck swung open, aided by a goblin, and everyone walked out onto a road. They were in the shadow of hills, with scrubby tumbleweed racing past. The skies were clear but for the most unusual aircraft ever seen: a cross between a winged helicopter and a mould-covered sausage, the utterly ridiculous goblinmobile came down to land.

THE MYTHICAL 9th DIVISION

Chapter 9: Over and Out

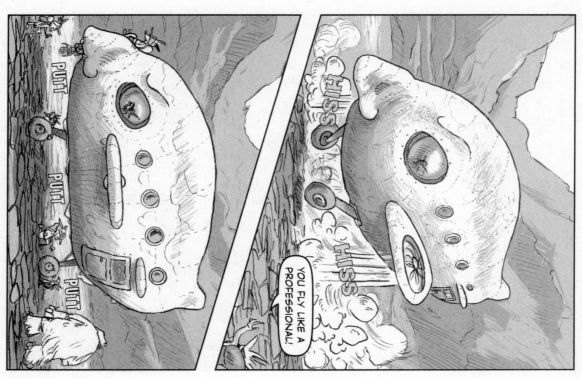

HE'S KIDDING, RIGHT?
NARG SPACECRAFT ARE MUCH CLEANER.
YOU FIRST, TIMONEN.

"**M**ake yourselves comfortable," said Grizzle.

Timonen bumped his head on the very low, soggy ceiling and a smear of yellowy gunge came off on his head.

"Comfortable?" he said. "I can't even stand up straight!"

It was dark green inside the vehicle, with soft wall panelling that appeared to be made of moss. There was a definite smell of damp about it, which made Albrecht think twice about sitting down.

"Please!" said Grizzle. He licked a seat and gestured for Albrecht to sit. "I have cleaned it for you!"

"Thanks," said Albrecht.

"And while we're on the subject," said Timonen, "what food have you got?"

Grizzle looked at the other goblins and they all snorted. One of them pointed to the wall panelling, giving Grizzle an awful idea.

"We are well stocked!" he lied, laughing terribly.

Grizzle squeezed past Saar and slid his hand down the helicopter wall. His fingers plucked four mushrooms that had previously been growing happily in the damp conditions.

"Here!" said Grizzle, throwing them in Timonen's direction. "Goblin speciality!"

Timonen looked at the meagre pickings and sniffed them. They smelled mushroomy with a touch of mouldy socks. Timonen tossed them into his mouth.

"Tastes of…" said Timonen, still working out what their flavour reminded him of. He chewed them and swallowed.

"…Granny toenails."

"URGH!" cried the goblins, before laughing at the top of their lungs.

Saar pushed Timonen with the end of his staff.

"You're disgusting," he said.

"What?" said Timonen. "I'm not gonna pass up a meal?"

A bright ringing noise rang out in the aircraft, and Grizzle picked up the brown plastic goblinphone. It was Captain Ponkerton.

"Here! Furry!" said Grizzle. "For you!"

"Captain!" exclaimed Albrecht, as he received the phone.

"How pleased am I to hear you?!"

"Where on Earth have you been?" exclaimed Ponkerton.

"We've not been on Earth, actually," said Albrecht, "but that's another story."

"Good grief," said Ponkerton.

"Grundy's gone mad," said Albrecht.

"WHAT?!" said Ponkerton.

"He's threatening to take over the world", said Albrecht.

"There's also a space monster about to attack Las Vegas."

Ponkerton tried to swallow all this information.

"Why haven't we seen this on the news?" he asked.

"He's probably blocked all comms," said Albrecht. "He's good at things like that."

"And is there anything else you should tell me?" he asked.

"We're surrounded by aliens…" said Albrecht.

"Okay," said Ponkerton. "I don't want to know any more."

"I'm sure there was something else," said Albrecht.

"No, that's plenty," said Ponkerton. "So what's Grundy's plan?"

"He's in possession of a metal-eating goop," said Albrecht.

"If it gets loose it could bring down civilization."

"You're absolutely right!" said Ponkerton. "No power lines, no computers, no bridges. It could be the end of the world as we know it."

"Exactly," said Albrecht.

"Then you have my orders to capture Solomon Grundy in whatever manner is necessary," said Ponkerton. "I'll inform LEGENDS command."

"And the space monster?" asked Albrecht.

"Do what you have to," said Ponkerton. "LEGENDS is operating blind on this, so we're relying on you. Don't let this maniac get his way."

The phone cut out.

"Looks like it's up to us," said Albrecht.

Grizzle fell silent, stood as straight as he could and saluted.

"To defend the Earth even if our lives are at risk," said Grizzle, recanting their division's pledge to LEGENDS. He then burst into fits of laughter, along with the whole of the goblin division.

"What's so funny?" said Albrecht.

"Everything," said Grizzle.

"I'm glad we've cleared that up then," said Albrecht.

Vast columns of vehicles were leaving Las Vegas by every available road. The traffic was one way, but for a convoy of Grundy's DECON team.

"We have it in sight!" said a soldier, clad from head to toe in black battle fatigues.

The armoured jeep swerved on the tarmac, blocking half of the freeway. The other half was clogged with cars and lorries, as the citizens of Las Vegas evacuated as quickly as they could. A huge pool of Nanogrime lay dormant on the dirt beside the road. A giant set of footprints were depressed into the ground nearby.

"Get ready to engage..." said the soldier.

He leapt from the jeep, followed by his team. All were ready for a battle. Grundy stepped out last, shielded by the open door, and tore off his eye patch. The monster was about a mile ahead, and he focused on the creature with his robotic eye.

"It's more than impressive," he said, as the monster tore an electricity pylon from the dry ground as though it was a dandelion. The monster crunched it between its massive jaws and swallowed it down in one gulp. A waterfall of Nanogrime flew out of its mouth, covering vehicles and buildings.

Las Vegas was seriously under attack.

"I want it alive, you hear me?" said Grundy. "Alive."

"We'll do everything in our power, sir," said the soldier. He made a series of hand gestures and the troops formed a protective cordon along the road.

The remaining vehicles of Grundy's DECON team reached his roadblock. He walked back towards them with his hand raised, and they stopped in good time.

"No further," ordered Grundy. "This is our perimeter. Anything metal past here will be too much of a lure for that monster."

"Captain!" said the driver of his jeep. "We've lost contact with the quarantine vehicle."

Grundy was furious.

"How?" he said.

"Unconfirmed," said the driver.

"Get me the facts," said Grundy. "The last thing we need is those yetis escaping."

"Yes, sir," replied the driver.

Grundy trained his eye on the space monster, calculating its strengths.

"How do you bring down a Goliath?" he asked himself.

"Big weapons."

"Sir?" said a soldier.

"Engage the Static Hyper Resistor," said Grundy. "Aim high."

A heavily-laden lorry was driven to the front line. It lowered six wide footplates to secure its balance and a large satellite dish rose up into the air from its flatbed. It was angled to face the monster.

Grundy gave the command, and an aching hum rippled through the air from the dish.

In Las Vegas, the unusual quiet was suddenly disturbed by an explosion of mobile phones. Televisions left playing in empty hotel rooms burst into flames, and every radio signal became indecipherable, clouded garbage.

The monster shook as it registered a tingling sensation in its head. The tingle became an irritation, forcing it to spit out a cement mixer it had been crunching. Then it saw the dish and Grundy's army.

"It has us in its sights," said a soldier.

"And the Hyper Resistor hasn't even stunned it," said Grundy.

"Captain!" shouted a soldier. "Helicopter incoming!"

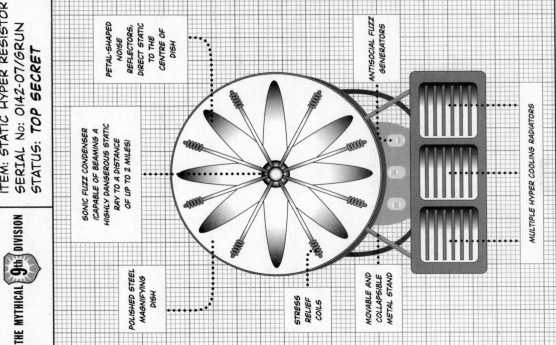

Grundy's attention switched to the sky.

"That's no helicopter," he said, spitting his words. "That's the goblinmobile of the Mythical 4th Division."

"What's our response, sir?" said the soldier.

"Sit tight," said Grundy, a slight smile forming on his lips. "They're about to enter the field of intensified static. It may not hurt the monster, but that helicopter won't like it one bit."

"Enemy in sight!" squealed Fizzle, the goblin pilot. "Climbing to jump height."

"Buckle up!" shouted Grizzle to his fellow goblins.

Albrecht squeezed his way across the craft and looked down at the monster from a window. It looked even larger than before, and from above he could see the details of its metallic skin reflecting the sun's rays. The city grid spread out into the distance, its grey buildings and green golf courses an oddity amongst the featureless desert.

"Any sign of Grundy?" asked Saar.

"There's a host of black vehicles on the city outskirts," said Albrecht.

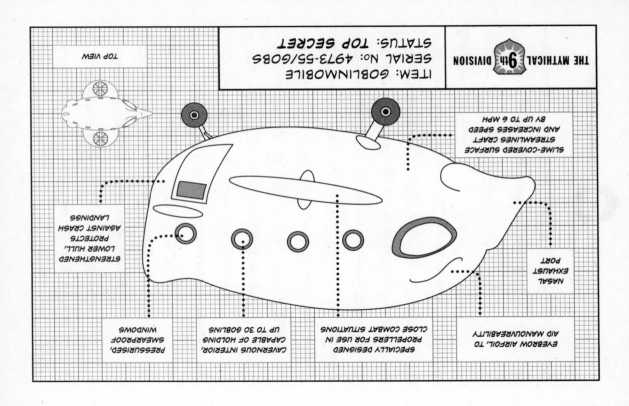

"He's avoiding direct contact with the monster," said Saar.

"That sounds sensible. Maybe we should do the same."

"Don't worry yourselves," said Grizzle. "You furballs sit tight."

"Eh?" said Timonen. "Who made him the boss?"

The goblins pushed their way through the helicopter to the door.

"Out the way," said Grizzle, bumping into Timonen's leg.

"Fizzle drives this thing. Talk to him if you want to land."

"Why? Where will you be?" asked Albrecht.

"Fighting," shouted Grizzle. "GOBLINS ATTACK!"

The head goblin slid open the door, and a gush of wind coursed inside. The goblins righted their goggles, shouted a few chants and ran out into the sky screaming their heads off. Albrecht peered through the door, holding on tight.

"They're absolutely mad," he said.

"What?!" said Timonen. "How come they get to have all the fun?"

The goblins were falling faster by the second, and were soon within grasp of the giant monster. Grizzle hadn't bargained on

its mouth being so large. The monster's head swayed back and forth trying to suck in the metal clasps of the parachutes.

"Take out his eyes!" screamed Grizzle.

Grizzle liked playing computer games and he knew eyes were always the weak spots of baddies.

The goblins landed on the monster's head, discharged their chutes and clung on with their fingers and toenails to stop them from slipping. The eyes were still far away, and its four hands slapped at its head trying to swat the goblins as though they were midges.

"Dastardly fingers!" cried Grizzle, who was dodging the dangerous digits for his life.

He crawled across the monster until he was securely gripping a giant monsterish eyebrow. He called his team to join him. With eight goblins at his side he prepared to strike.

"NOW WE EAT!" he shouted defiantly, and with a terrific cry of intent, the goblins chomped down into the monster's flesh.

Grizzle hadn't bargained on the flesh being as hard as iron. Goblins are great at chewing through sheet metal and cables, but when it comes to steel girders, that's another thing entirely.

The goblins' teeth chimed like bells against the skin. Their heads froze as shockwaves ran up through their jaws, into their eyeballs and out through the tips of their pointy ears.

"Waaaaargh!" screamed Grizzle.

When his ears had stopped ringing, he realized there was another strange sound to be heard over the crunching metal noises emanating from the monster.

The goblinmobile, a long way above his head was spluttering smoke from its exhaust. There was something very wrong going on.

"Fizzle!" he cried, shaking his fist. "I envy you!"

The aircraft started to buzz, and Fizzle pressed every button and control at his disposal.

"Looking like a goblin mash-up," said Fizzle. "All systems crash. We've got a smash coming on, boss!"

"Did he just say we were going to crash?" Saar didn't like what he was hearing.

"I say smash," said Fizzle, ecstatically. "Very soon!"

"Fleas of a yak," said Albrecht.

"We are used to crashes," said Oola.

The Narg gripped each other's hands.

"We're going to die," said Timonen.

"No we're not," said Albrecht. "Fizzle, do something."

Fizzle left the controls and appeared at Albrecht's side.

"What are you doing?" asked Albrecht.

"Something," said Fizzle, wearing a terrifyingly mad smile.

The helicopter's rotors stopped abruptly and the craft plummeted Earthwards.

"We're going to die," said Albrecht.

Chapter 10: Viva Las Vegas

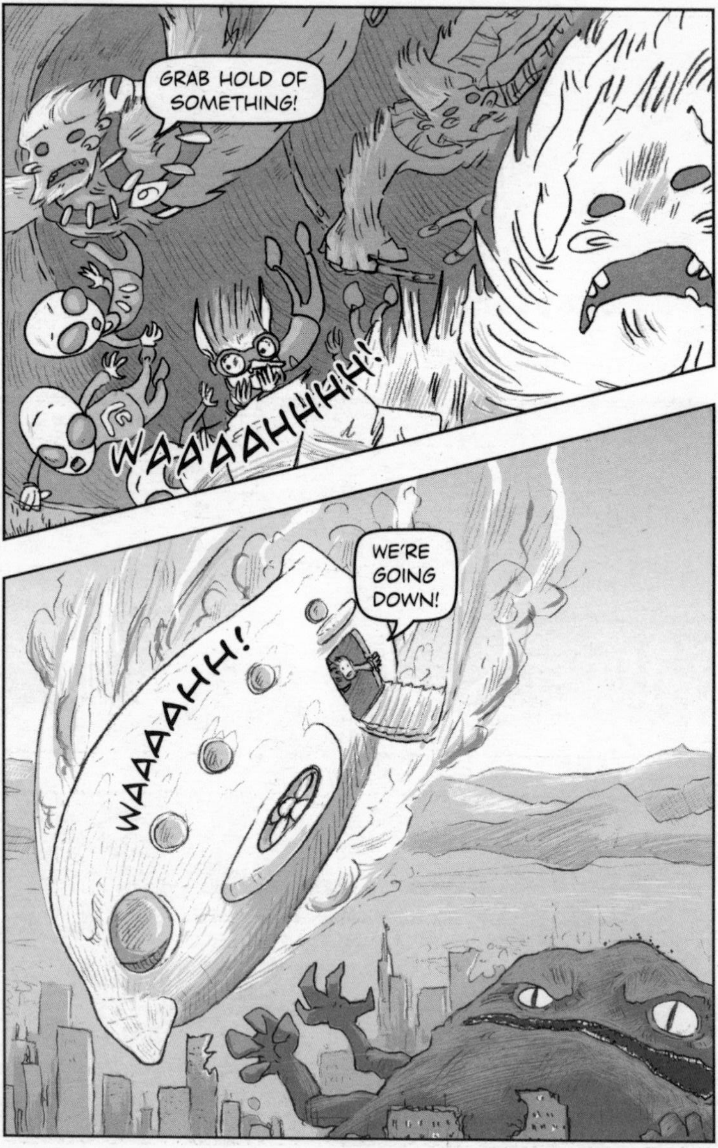
GRAB HOLD OF SOMETHING!
WAAAAHHHH!
WE'RE GOING DOWN!
WAAAAAHH!

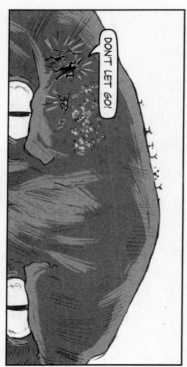

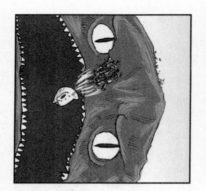

"It's eaten the goblinmobile," said a soldier.

"I can see that," said Grundy.

"But I can also see those yeti vermin on the creature's head."

"We have numerous snipers," said the soldier. "We could take them out from the ground?"

"Focus on the monster," said Grundy. "It's heading our way." He

was growing steadily aware that his plan to secure the monster alive was hopeful at best. It was just too strong.

"Yes, sir," said a soldier. "We can have jets overhead in forty-five seconds. Armour piercing shells should do it."

"Forty-five seconds is too long," said Grundy. "But call them in anyway."

"Yes, sir."

Grundy thought about their situation. The lowering sun was now directly behind the monster and cast a distant shadow over the land.

"Weaken the ground beneath it," said Grundy. "Aim our Groundshakers into the earth. We need to destabilize it."

"Yes, sir," said the soldier. "Should we worry about collateral damage?"

"No," he replied.

Grundy couldn't have cared less.

"This plan of yours," said Saar, clinging onto the monster's head. "It was never going to work, was it?"

"You mock goblins?!" said Grizzle, angrily.

"I wouldn't say 'mock,'" offered Albrecht. "More..."

He thought furiously, delving deep for the answer.

"... your plan wasn't fully thought through."

The monster was taking them rapidly across Las Vegas towards Grundy and his DECON team.

"We'll show you!" cried Grizzle. "Goblins ATTACK!"

Once again the goblins bit into the monster, and once again their teeth chimed off its skin. The monster felt nothing.

"My teeth are weak!" cried Grizzle with frustration. He was very angry with them and tried to pull them out.

"Stop that," pleaded Albrecht. A goblin removing his own teeth was enough to make even a yeti squeamish.

Grizzle spat on the monster's head in disgust.

"We need a better plan than just eating this thing," said Albrecht.

"Hang about," said Saar, "they're up to something on the ground."

He pointed to Grundy, who they could now see with their own eyes. A rocket launcher fired high into the sky, and four fat missiles soared into the stratosphere only to come down punishingly fast. The ground exploded beneath the monster, and an earthquake shook the outer suburbs of the city. The monster was thrown off-balance and it tumbled down, jettisoning the Narg, yetis and goblins onto the freeway. The monster smashed into the ground a few hundred metres from Grundy's DECON team, wiping out a whole suburb.

The yetis protected the Narg as the monster's arms flailed around. Despite their dangerous position, the goblins were in fits of laughter on the ground.

"What is it with you lot?" asked Saar.

The monster's fingers were clawing either side of him, helping it to get back on its feet.

"You wait!" cried Grizzle. "Goblins now have the know-how to fell this beast!"

He removed his backpack and goggles, which were battered from the fall, and threw them to the ground.

"Goblins!" he shouted, while dancing in the shadow of the monster's raised foot. "Prepare for attack number three!"

The goblins twirled around excitedly.

"Fleas of a yak," said Saar. "What is it this time?"

"Goblin power move," said Grizzle, laughing loudly. "You won't mock us soon!"

The goblins ran off excitedly, yipping and squealing aloud.

"In fairness to them," said Albrecht, "they certainly have guts."

"And determination," added Saar.

"Get me the yeti," said Grundy, who was passed a communicator. Albrecht's RoAR beeped and Grundy was connected.

"Are you still alive?" asked Grundy, surveying the monster as it tried to regain balance.

Albrecht withdrew the RoAR from his backpack.

"Of course I am," he said.

Grundy threw the communicator to the ground in a fit of anger. He quickly picked it back up again, dusting off the dirt before placing it beside his ear.

"Then start saying your prayers," he spat. "Our fighters rarely miss."

The skies rumbled with the sound of jet engines, and Grundy's eyes followed the fighter planes as they swept down the valley. A barrage of armour-piercing missiles detached from their wings and soared across the city, targeting the mighty monster.

"It will take more than luck to survive that," said Grundy.

"Incoming!" shouted Albrecht.

Amidst the wreckage of the Las Vegas suburb, he pointed out the jet planes zooming in.

"Get behind the monster!" shouted Saar.

Timonen threw a load of Narg onto his shoulders and dragged the rest with his hands.

They slipped into the crater left by the monster and, as three

rockets exploded onto the monster's back, they were shielded from the blast. The monster treated the rockets as a mere inconvenience. It brushed off its back and returned its focus to Grundy.

The monster was ready to move again. It raised its body into the air by its spindly legs, and bellowed the most enormous roar.

"Can nothing stop this thing?" asked Saar.

"GOBLINS CAN!" cried Grizzle, returning to Albrecht.

The goblins had toppled a lengthy row of overhead power lines and dragged the cables, still sparking with electricity, towards the monster.

"WATCH!" shouted Grizzle.

The Goblins ran around the monster's feet, looping power cables around its ankles. As it moved, the cables tightened.

"Well I never," said Saar.

"They've done it!" said Albrecht.

The monster's giant head dipped to the floor and burped a metallic burp as it caught sight of the goblins. It swiped an oil tanker in their direction, but could do nothing to stop itself toppling over like a felled giant redwood.

* * *

Grundy's face was rapidly obscured by shadow. The monster was falling in his direction, its mouth wide and its teeth bared.

He darted behind his armoured jeep and crouched low as the monster slammed into the ground. It wiped out most of his DECON team, crushing vehicles and cyborg soldiers to a pulp under its enormous weight. Grundy was lucky enough to have been positioned in one of the monster's four armpits.

He stood up, imprisoned by a wall of metal skin. Anger bubbled out of his mouth.

"This was not how I envisaged this afternoon playing out," he said.

"Sir," said the driver, who was sheltering under the vehicle. "Is it dead?"

The ground shook, and a ripple ran across the monster's skin. It roared aloud in preparation for clambering to its feet.

"There's your answer," said Grundy.

"They almost showed some brains then," said Saar.

The yetis ran down the freeway, eventually reaching the band of goblins, who were laughing louder than ever before.

"You mock us!" said Grizzle. "See what we do! Monster is STUPID!"

He was pointing at one of the monster's huge, unmoving feet.

"It looks like you've stunned it," said Albrecht.

Suddenly the monster's toes stretched out. It lifted its heel and then, using all four hands, dragged itself up. A whole canyon had been scratched into the earth.

The monster roared into the sky.

"It looks angry," said Saar.

"Angrier," said Albrecht.

The monster pulled at the cables around its feet. It tore them to pieces and cast the remnants into its mouth. It stared down at its attackers. The fire in its eyes was refuelled and burned brighter.

"We have truly angered it," said Oola.

Albrecht saw a lone jeep standing under the monster. A man in a black suit was at its side.

"Grundy..." he said.

"I think he's quite upset," said Timonen.

"Wouldn't you be?" said Saar. "Imagine if your plans for world domination were flattened under a monster."

Grundy was suddenly obscured by the monster's foot. It had caught hold of a new scent and was on the move back into the centre of Las Vegas. Its arms swept down across the ground, narrowly missing the crowd of goblins.

"Here it comes again," shouted Albrecht. "Run!"

Timonen hurled Oola under his arm and the whole group ran for the city. The monster lunged at them, swatting away anything that got in its path. Its feet trampled over houses and gardens leaving massive footprints in the ground. Its hands reached out, hitting the road in front of the yetis. They leaped onto them, only to jump off the other side and continue running.

They darted from block to block, heading further downtown.

The sun was setting over the hills and neon lights were kicking into life all around. Even though Las Vegas had been evacuated, the city was still alive – but for how much longer, it was hard to tell.

"Follow them," said Grundy, commanding his driver.

"We are outnumbered," said the driver. "It may not be in

our best interests."

Grundy took one look at the cyborg and pushed him through the door and out onto the road.

"I have no time for imbeciles," he said.

He slid onto the driver's seat and started the engine.

"I just want to destroy those yetis," he said, feverishly shunting the gears.

The yetis ran to the edge of a bridge crossing the freeway and ducked behind a row of abandoned cars. The Narg were close behind, but the goblins had another hare-brained scheme and had run off towards a casino, its lights flashing like fireworks.

"Where are they going?" he said, sighing.

"Let's let them do their thing," said Saar.

"I don't have the energy for this any more," said Albrecht. "I feel like I've been awake for a week."

"We need Powershakes," said Timonen.

"You need nothing of the sort," said Saar.

Albrecht weighed up the situation.

"Oola," he said seriously, "I want the Narg to find cover here. From now on it'll be us yetis that do the running."

Oola shook her head.

"Whatever happens," she said. "I will fight with you."

"I'll protect the little Nargies," said Timonen. "I can nearly fit them all on top of my head."

"Of course you can help us, Oola," said Albrecht, ignoring Timonen. "But the rest of the Narg should stay here. We didn't rescue them from the Moon just for your race to be wiped out as soon as we landed."

"You have an interplanetary deal," said Oola. "Our alliance shall be a strong one."

"So, any bright ideas?" said Saar.

"I think the goblins had the right approach," said Albrecht. "Bringing the monster down to our level."

"But then what?" said Saar. "That beast is impervious to everything."

Albrecht peered out from the bridge and spotted the courageous, if mad, goblins trotting down the street.

"Maybe they know something we don't?" he said.

Grizzle led his comrades down the Las Vegas strip. Huge casinos, recreated world landmarks and walls of neon lights lined the road. Not that the goblins cared: they were high on the thrill of battle, cackling and jeering aloud.

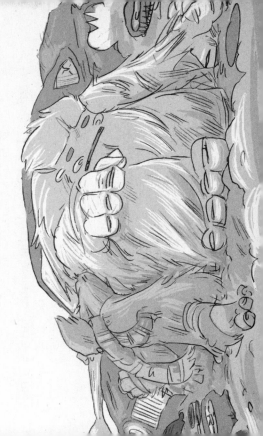

The monster was enjoying mouthfuls of steel, tearing the tops off buildings and sending them to the scrapyard of its stomach. And with each mouthful it stepped nearer to its enemies. It had always kept an eye on their whereabouts and was not letting them slip.

"Goblin attack number three!" cried Grizzle.

The goblins stopped dead.

"Three?" they said dully. "We've done three!"

"AHA!" announced Grizzle. "But this time we also add attack number four!"

"Four!?" squealed the goblins. They couldn't control their excitement. "What is attack number four?"

"WE LIGHT IT UP!" cried Grizzle. Foam bubbled from the side of his mouth.

"Grizzle is MAD!" squealed the goblins. "Grizzle is the BEST!"

The monster stepped over the boulevard and pulled a hotel clear of its foundations. Cables and pipes flopped to the ground from its lower floors and water mains burst sending fountains into the sky. The monster took bites out of the hotel like it was a piece of cake. A neon sign from the hotel's roof clattered to the ground and sent a shower of sparks over the goblins.

"Electric rain!" screamed the goblins, basking in the glow.

"ATTACK!"

The goblins ran as fast as they could towards the monster. They found as many exposed power cables as they could, dragged them out of the ground and once again wrapped them around the monster's feet.

"NEVER GIVE UP!" screamed Grizzle excitedly. "THE MONSTER IS STUPID!"

Once the trap was set, the goblins regrouped, and set about phase two of their plan.

Albrecht watched Grizzle and his team hurriedly drag cables, tightening them about the monster's legs. The monster tossed the few remaining floors of the hotel to one side, and started to rock left and right. Its balance was faltering and before it could remove the new ties around its ankles, it fell to the ground once more. It crashed through a massive hotel complex and its head fell smack bang right into the middle of a huge rollercoaster ride.

The goblins cheered.

"Must act fast!" shouted Grizzle.

"That's our cue," said Albrecht. "They may need our help."

The yetis charged to the goblins.

"We're with you!" shouted Albrecht.

Grizzle squealed.

"Now goblins light up monster like Christmas tree!" he said.

THE MYTHICAL 9th DIVISION

Chapter 11: Bright Sparks

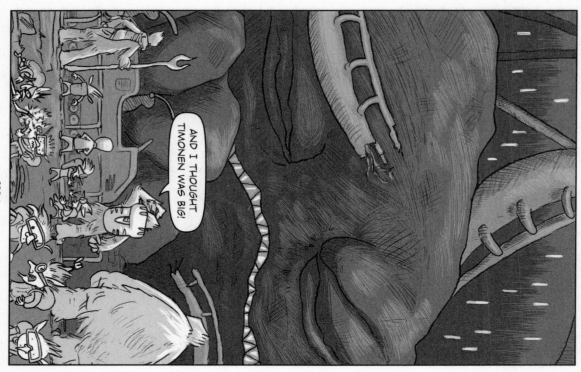

"O f course!" said Saar. "Metals combine as alloys to form supermetals."

"Stupid Narg," said Oola. "We should have seen this ourselves!"

"Let's hope the goblins find enough power to make it work," said Albrecht.

The goblins were fiddling with a power junction that ran the rollercoaster, attempting to electrify the rails of

the ride. They were planning to fry the monster as it lay stunned. Unfortunately, the monster decided it wasn't going to be stunned any longer. Its eyes flicked open.

"Guys," said Timonen. "It's awake."

The monster groaned and thought about moving. Its massive eyes blinked.

"We have to keep the monster occupied," said Albrecht.

"I was fearing you might say that," said Saar.

"We need to bait the line," said Albrecht.

Saar looked at the rollercoaster cars parked up beside them.

"You thinking what I'm thinking?" said Saar.

"Oh boy," said Albrecht, laughing. "It's been nice knowing you."

"We're going for a ride?" said Timonen. "YES!"

Albrecht ran his eyes over the track.

"It's broken in three places," said Albrecht. "We'll have to jump."

"Should buy the goblins some time, though," said Saar.

"Exactly," said Albrecht. "SORT THE POWER!" he shouted to Grizzle. "WE'LL KEEP THE MONSTER BUSY."

"You are thinking like true goblins!" cried Grizzle waving his hands in the air. "YOU ARE OFFICIALLY MAD!"

The yetis jumped into the rollercoaster cars and got comfortable. This was going to be quite a ride.

"Plastic interior," said Saar. "That's a relief."

"Don't touch the sides," said Albrecht, "just in case."

Oola found a seat and pulled down the safety bar to lock herself in place.

"The Narg will see this to the end," she said.

"When you're ready," shouted Albrecht.

Timonen rubbed his hands in excitement.

Grizzle pulled a lever and the rollercoaster started up. The carriage was pulled high up a sloping track, and seconds later

the yetis were in line with the monster's frowning eyebrows. The rollercoaster slowed. The monster opened its mouth, revealing a row of teeth the size of Timonen.

The track wrapped its way around the monster, with broken sections at each side of its body. The ride was just beginning.

"Hold tight!" said Albrecht.

The carriage reached the apex of the slope, and the only way was down.

The car soared down at such an alarming rate that the monster's eyes blinked in shock. It lifted its head high and pulled one of its hands to its side, following the course of the track, and the yetis, with a finger. It was getting ready to squash them.

"GRIZZLE!" shouted Albrecht.

The monster crushed the track with its finger, but missed the carriage by a mile, it was moving far too quickly.

Timonen screamed with delight as they dipped and twisted high into the air, navigating a serious loop.

Grizzle diverted the power, and with the monster's body still caught up in the track, it was trapped in a surge of energy. The rollercoaster looped the loop, and the monster jerked

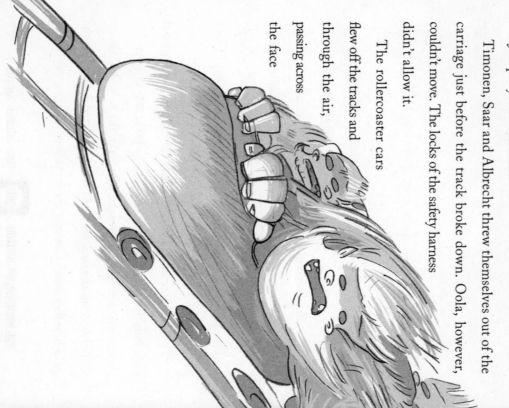

into the air, its body glowing bright white as electricity jolted through it. Sparks leaped from its hands.

"Jump!" yelled Albrecht.

Timonen, Saar and Albrecht threw themselves out of the carriage just before the track broke down. Oola, however, couldn't move. The locks of the safety harness didn't allow it.

The rollercoaster cars flew off the tracks and through the air, passing across the face

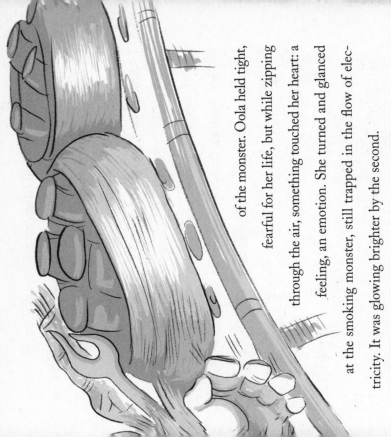

of the monster. Oola held tight, fearful for her life, but while zipping through the air, something touched her heart: a feeling, an emotion. She turned and glanced at the smoking monster, still trapped in the flow of electricity. It was glowing brighter by the second.

When the carriage hit the ground it buckled and twisted. Oola was protected from harm by the safety bar, but her body was battered as it slid over the ground like a plastic snake. Eventually the carriage smashed into a wall.

The monster reared up onto its legs. It had fought off the attack and won.

"Did we get it?" said Albrecht.

Saar opened his eyes and saw the monster bearing down on them. Its body twinkled with the remaining electrical charge leaving its body.

"No, is your answer," said Saar.

"NOT HOT ENOUGH!" shouted Grizzle. He was seething with rage. Attack number four hadn't worked.

The goblins reached the yetis just as the monster tore the rollercoaster track from its foundations and ate it. Clots of Nanogrime were spat out over the city. Then the monster saw the carriage lying helplessly on the ground. It picked it up with one hand and dangled it high above its mouth like a string of spaghetti.

"Oola!" said Albrecht.

"Oh no?!" said Timonen. "My little Nargie's still on board."

"And that's where she's going to stay," said Grundy, a twinkle of madness in his eye.

Solomon Grundy was stood behind the yetis bearing a huge Electrobolt Laser gun. He fired it at the monster, and a bright white bolt of electricity surged into the metallic beast. If nothing else, it got the creature's attention.

The yetis braced themselves. Timonen walked forward.

"Don't move another step," said Grundy. "You've seen what this can do."

"After everything we've been through today," said Saar, "you're the least of our worries."

"You can't escape," said Albrecht.

"I don't want to escape," said Grundy. "I want to destroy you."

Albrecht spotted his robotic eye.

"What's that in your head?" he said.

"The eye?" said Grundy. "One of the perks of working in Compound W. I have a cyborgian skull. My brain works three times as fast as yours."

"Who cares about brains," said Timonen, "when you have muscles like these."

The monster groaned and caught everyone's attention once more. It shook its head, and continued lowering the roller-coaster carriages. It dangled each car into its mouth and sucked them, one by one, as though it were covered in sauce. It was enjoying the moment.

"Oola..." said Albrecht.

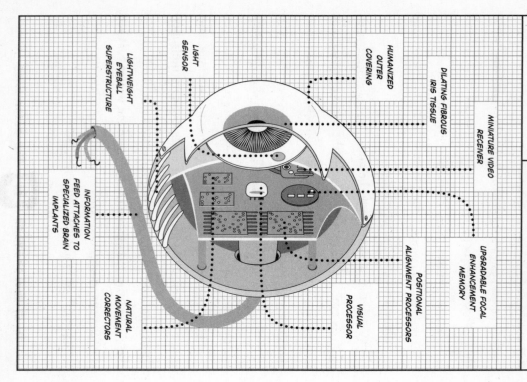

THE MYTHICAL **9th** DIVISION

ITEM: ROBOTIC EYE
SERIAL No: 0153-16/GRUN
STATUS: **TOP SECRET**

LIGHTWEIGHT EYEBALL SUPERSTRUCTURE

LIGHT SENSOR

HUMANIZED OUTER COVERING

DILATING FIBROUS IRIS TISSUE

MINIATURE VIDEO RECEIVER

INFORMATION FEED ATTACHES TO SPECIALIZED BRAIN IMPLANTS

NATURAL MOVEMENT CORRECTORS

VISUAL PROCESSOR

POSITIONAL ALIGNMENT PROCESSORS

UPGRADABLE FOCAL ENHANCEMENT MEMORY

Grundy laughed evilly.

"I'll let you watch the Narg die first, then I'll take my time over you," he said.

But the monster's eyes flashed bright pink and swelled to even more massive proportions. The earth shook – the monster being the epicentre of the quake – and a giant mushroom cloud billowed from its mouth.

"What on Earth was that?" said Albrecht.

Everyone turned to face the monster. Its bulging stomach rippled, contorted, then contracted and a fountain of Nanogrime blasted out over the yetis, the goblins and Grundy.

The monster's body darkened, and a thin tree of white veins spread over its skin. With a thunderous roar its mouth froze and the final three carriages fell limply down, caught on a row of its teeth.

Albrecht cleared Nanogrime from his face in order to breathe. He rapidly cleaned off his backpack, but it seemed a futile task. There would be holes through it in minutes.

"The monster's stopped moving," said Saar, wiping his eyes.

"Monster's dead," said Grizzle, swimming to the top of the Nanogrime sea. "MONSTER'S DEAD!"

"Surely not," said Saar.

Grundy wrestled himself free of the Nanogrime. He frantically tried to fire the Electrobolt at the yetis, but it was drowned in the goop. His eye started to twitch, and he dropped his weapon.

"Not so strong now, are you?!" said Timonen. He waded over to Grundy, only for the man to start shielding his face.

"What is it?" said Timonen, tapping him on the head with one of his chunky fingers.

Grundy started screaming.

"It's eating me!" he cried. "My eye!"

"That'll teach you to have a metal brain," said Timonen.

"Have some mercy," said Saar.

Timonen huffed.

Grundy was scratching furiously at his head. The Nanogrime had got to work immediately, eating through his robotic eye and chewing through into his skull.

"Leave him," said Albrecht.

Grundy pulled himself from the goop in a fit of agony. He didn't get far before he collapsed into a heap and died.

Chapter 12: The Eagle has Landed

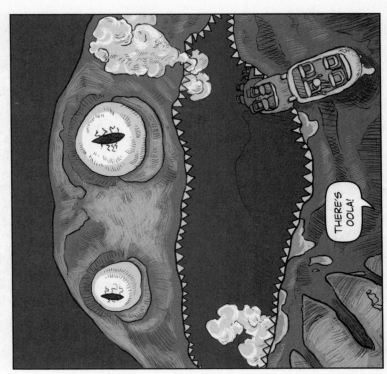

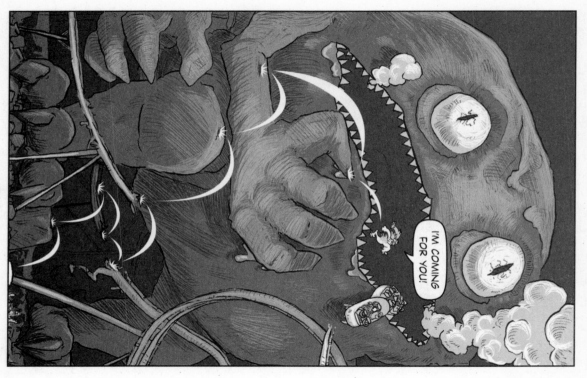

217

"What happened up there?" asked Albrecht.

Oola caught her breath.

"It was Tala," she said.

"Your ship?" said Albrecht. "But the monster ate all that was left of her."

"It was her heart," said Oola. "The Vuranium at her heart remained powerful."

"It remained inside the monster?" asked Saar.

"The metal casing of the orb was built to contain nuclear fuel," said Oola. "It is also capable of self-destructing. I heard Tala's voice when I flew through the air. She called to me with her last breaths, asking if she could help."

"She gave her life to save yours," said Saar.

"And the nuclear blast created enough heat to melt the metals in the monster," said Albrecht. "Turning it into this great lump."

Albrecht kicked one of the monster's toes.

"Incredible," said Saar.

"How come we weren't affected by the blast?" said Timonen.

"I thought nukes were bad for us?"

"Tala told me of the metals within the monster," said Oola.

"There was enough lead to shield us."

Grizzle marched over to Albrecht. He spat on his palm and shook the yeti's hand.

"We're off," said Grizzle.

"It's been interesting," said Albrecht.

"No!" cheered Grizzle. "It's been horrible."

The goblins ran away, laughing and squealing into the debris that was Las Vegas. Albrecht still didn't know what to think of them.

"I suppose we should be getting you back to base," said Albrecht to Oola. "It's been quite a day."

"The Narg are safe once more," said Oola. "Though now even further from home. Without a craft we are forever Earth-bound."

"You can always come stay with me," said Timonen. "I have a cave."

"The Mighty Fluff is very kind," said Oola. "But the Narg need a different planet."

"Shame," said Timonen.

Helicopters buzzed overhead, and searchlights whizzed across

the damaged city. Under their protection, the yetis and the Narg walked back through the deserted and desolate streets. Roulette wheels from shattered casinos littered the roads and poker chips blocked drains. Neon lights flickered on broken signposts.

"We didn't do too much damage, did we?" said Albrecht.

"It could have been a lot worse," said Timonen.

"That's the spirit," said Saar.

"So strictly speaking," said Albrecht, sitting outside Compound W with the Sherpa standing by ready for take-off, "none of this ever happened?"

"That's right," said Ponkerton, his face clear on the RoAR's screen. "And a new Solomon Grundy is in place at the 7th Division.

"A new Grundy?" said Albrecht.

"It's always been a codename," said Ponkerton. "Top secret, of course."

"And how are the press covering this?" asked Albrecht.

"It was an advertising stunt for a new casino and roller-coaster ride," said Ponkerton.

"I see," said Albrecht. "And the Nanogrime has been cleaned up?"

"We've seen to that," said Ponkerton.

"And the monster?"

"Once the city is rebuilt, it's likely to become a huge tourist attraction," said Ponkerton. "It's now the tallest building in the world."

"At least something good has come of it," said Albrecht.

"But don't forget," said Ponkerton, "the aliens are top secret. The world is not ready to know about them."

"The secrets will stay with us," said Albrecht.

"Good!" said Ponkerton. "I can always rely on you."

"Always," said Albrecht.

"So what was the Moon like?" asked Ponkerton. "I've had dreams of being a spaceman all my life."

"Sorry?" said Albrecht. "What Moon?"

"The one you just visited," he replied.

Saar tapped on the window of Sherpa I, he was keen to get home to the Himalayas.

"Honestly," said Albrecht with a twinkle in his eye, "I don't know what you mean."

"But you just…" said Ponkerton, tailing off awkwardly.

Albrecht smiled and saluted.

"I'll be seeing you soon, sir," he said. "Over and out!"

223

WOW!

IN HONOUR OF OUR FURRY SAVIOURS, WE SHALL NAME HER YETI.

THAT WAY THE NARG WILL NEVER FORGET YOUR KINDNESS.

SHE IS BEAUTIFUL.

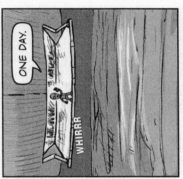

225

THE
END

Appendix: The Founding of the Mythical 7th Division

The Mythical 7th Division has always been shrouded in secrecy. There are no recorded facts or dates relating to it within LEGENDS' archives and, until fairly recently, very few people knew of its existence, let alone its specific role (if, indeed, it has one) within the organization.

In 1966, a leaked US governmental document linked a top secret military facility and a man named Solomon Grundy to a mysterious organization allied to the United Nations. After a huge uproar within LEGENDS high command, it was disclosed that Grundy was, in fact, the head of the Mythical 7th Division. No other facts were forthcoming, and the matter was hastily closed.

Over the years, conspiracy theorists within LEGENDS have linked the Mythical 7th Division to a number of unexplained incidents. In Siberia in 1908, a huge blast, far greater than an atomic bomb, flattened an estimated 80 million trees covering 2,150 square kilometres in Tunguska.

A contemporary artist's impression of the devastation cause by the blast.

RAAF Captures Flying Saucer On Ranch in Roswell Region

No Details of Crashed Craft Released

Movies Stop Moving

Kittens Found to Have The Cure For Cancer

Press cutting from the Roswell Recorder, 1947

People link the event to alien weaponry or spacecraft, and it has long been hinted that the Mythical 7th Division also had a role to play in the Roswell Incident of 1947. Unfortunately, because of the top secret nature of the Division, it is unlikely we shall ever know for sure what the Mythical 7th Division really is.

ALEX MILWAY HAS always enjoyed making up stories and, after leaving art college, he discovered that he liked to write and illustrate them as well. His interest in furry creatures first reared its head in the *MOUSEHUNTER* trilogy, where weird and wonderful mice ran riot all over the world. With *THE MYTHICAL 9TH DIVISION*, the fur quota got even bigger, as he had to master the art of drawing a troop of yetis whose main purpose was to save the world. Alex is now a full-time author-illustrator, who suffers from furballs and works from his home in London.

9th

OPERATION ROBOT STORM

TERROR OF THE DEEP

ALEX MILWAY

MYTHICAL 9th DIVISION

INCLUDES TOP-SECRET L.E.G.E.N.D.S. DOSSIER!

Armed, dangerous and covered in fur!

TERROR OF THE DEEP

THE YETIS' SECOND ADVENTURE
SEES THEM IN DEEP WATER...

978-1-4063-1800-5

WWW.WALKER.CO.UK

WWW.MYTHICAL9TH.COM

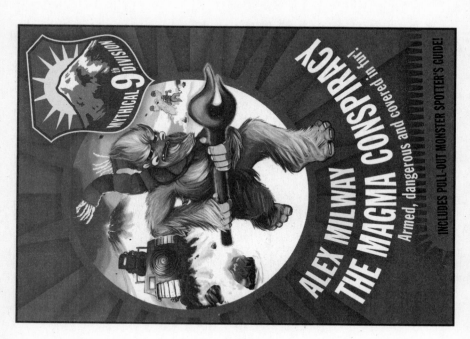